North Wall

For John and Brian, good friends living and dead

North Wall

Climbing the Alps' most demanding mountain

ROGER HUBANK

Vertebrate Publishing, Sheffield
www.v-publishing.co.uk

North Wall

Roger Hubank

 Vertebrate Publishing
Omega Court, 352 Cemetery Road, Sheffield S11 8FT, United Kingdom.
www.v-publishing.co.uk

First published in 1978 by The Viking Press, New York. This digital edition first
published in 2019 by Vertebrate Digital, an imprint of Vertebrate Publishing.

Vertebrate Publishing
Omega Court, 352 Cemetery Road, Sheffield S11 8FT

This book is a work of fiction. The names, characters, places, events and
incidents are products of the author's imagination. Any resemblance to actual
persons, living or dead, or actual events are purely coincidental.

A CIP catalogue record for this book is available from the British Library.

ISBN 978-1-912560-56-1 (ebook)
ISBN 978-1-912560-57-8 (paperback)

Every effort has been made to obtain the necessary permissions with
reference to copyright material, both illustrative and quoted. We apologise
for any omissions in this respect and will be pleased to make the appropriate
acknowledgements in any future edition.

Produced by Vertebrate Publishing.

'In this narrative we do more than record our adventures, we bear witness: events that seem to make no sense may sometimes have a deep significance of their own. There is no other justification for an *acte gratuit*.'

M. HERZOG, *Annapurna* 1950

Contents

Foreword

North Wall reflects a period in alpine climbing over half-a-century ago, as the description of the gear will soon make plain to those who know about such things. It is set in the Bregaglia, on the Swiss-Italian border. The village of 'Molino' is, in fact, Promontogno, at the foot of the Piz Badile, one of the six great north faces of the Alps. The peak on which the action takes place must have been sufficiently like the real thing for at least one prominent alpinist I know of to claim to have climbed the route described in the 'topo' – the *direttissima* on the north-east face of the Piz Molino. Though in fact the 'Piz Molino' doesn't exist. It's purely imaginary – constructed by John Brailsford and myself from bits and pieces of other mountains with its principal crux, the great 100-metre *dièdre*, lifted from the west face of the Dru.

Like many first novels *North Wall* contains a certain autobiographical element. It was Tony Whittome, my editor at Hutchinson, who persuaded me that the characters should be French rather than English, lest the originals be too recognizable. It was written at a time when my personal life was undergoing a purgatory of slow disintegration. Though I was certain of one thing: my time in the mountains was coming to an end. Even though, after an interval of some years, I did return to climbing, it was never again to be in the Alps. The book was originally called *The North Wall Candidate*, a title reflecting the immense admiration I felt for certain men I mingled with – far, far better climbers than myself. A kind of hero-worship, I suppose. Or else the siren call of a larger form of life, something beyond the familial, the domestic. The small man, as he was called then, was the first of my fictive heroes who went out in search of that further life only to discover that he was re-begot, as John Donne puts it, '*of absence, darkness, death: things that are not.*'

My later books were to rehearse the same theme repeatedly (it was Graham Greene who said we write the same novel over and over again): the allure of that further world set against the price it may exact; disillusion, the loss of innocence, and a sombre understanding that all our mysticisms of heroism end in self-estrangement.

The writer David Roberts, one of the outstanding modern chroniclers of the mountain life, won the Boardman Tasker award in 2018 with *Limits of the Known*. At the time of writing a dying man, he reveals in the final passage that what he wishes for in his last conscious moment before the light finally goes out, '… *is not the shining memory of some summit underfoot that I was the first to reach, not the gleam of yet another undiscovered land on the horizon,*' but the touch of his wife's fingers as she clasps his hand in hers, unwilling to let go.

That would be my wish too.

Roger Hubank.
Loughborough 2018

Glossary

Arête *(Fr.)* A sloping ridge of rock.

Belay *(to belay)* A method, used by climbers, of protecting themselves and their companions, by attaching the rope to a piton, or to a sling fastened to or around a suitable projection. There are many different methods of belaying.

Bergschrund *(Gr.)* A crevasse separating a glacier from the rock walls enclosing it, or from higher snow or ice fields.

Bivouac sack A simple, sack-like tent (minus poles) suspended from pitons fixed in the rock. In the mid-sixties it would have been regarded as something of a luxury.

Bridging A method of climbing whereby the climber makes use of holds on (and thereby 'bridges') adjacent rock faces.

Cagoule *(Fr.)* A long, waterproof overgarment.

Chimney A (usually vertical) fissure wide enough to admit the climber's body.

Cornice A potentially unstable mass of snow and ice overhanging a ridge.

Couloir *(Fr.)* Usually a steep gully, often containing snow, ice or loose rock. Like cornices, couloirs can form one of the objective hazards of mountaineering.

Crampon *(Fr.)* A framework of steel spikes strapped to the boot.

Crux A crucial point of difficulty in a climb. It may be a particular pitch, or even a single move.

Descendeur *(Fr.)* An implement to which the rope is attached during a rappel. It assists the climber to slide down the rope.

Dièdre *(Fr.)* An open, V-shaped corner.

Duvet A padded, down-filled jacket.

Étrier *(Fr.)* A short stirrup constructed of nylon line and two or three aluminium rungs. Étriers can be attached to pitons and used as artificial footholds on holdless rock.

Glacis An easy-angled, rock slope.

Glissade *(Fr.)* A controlled slide down snow slopes. A sort of skiing – sans skis.

Golo A metal wedge.

Jam To climb cracks by wedging hands (sometimes arms) and feet in the rocks.

Karabiner *(Gr.)* A steel or aluminium alloy snaplink. It can be used to attach the rope to the climber or, in conjunction with a piton or sling, to provide a 'running belay' to protect a falling leader.

Layback A method (extremely strenuous) of climbing a crack, in which the hands grip the rock edge (a sharp edge is virtually essential), the feet are pressed against the rock wall, and the body is lifted by pressure against the feet.

Mantelshelf A manoeuvre whereby the climber hoists himself on to a narrow ledge (often backed by a steep wall).

Névé *(Fr.)* Old, hard crystalline snow.

Pendule *(Fr.)* A manoeuvre whereby the climber makes a pendulum swing on the rope across a holdless wall.

Perlon A particular kind of nylon rope. Known for its strength, elasticity and ease of handling.

Pied d'éléphant *(Fr.)* A short, usually hip-length sleeping bag. Used in conjunction with a duvet.

Pitch A section of a climb between two stances.

Piton *(Fr.)* Steel or aluminium alloy spikes. They come in various shapes and sizes.

Prusik clip A locking device which, when attached to the rope, assists the climber to ascend the rope rather than the rock.

Rappel *(Fr.)* A method of lowering oneself down steep faces on a doubled rope.

Roof A large overhang, in which the rock projects forward almost horizontally (like a ceiling), is called a roof.

Runner *(Running-belay)* A method of using karabiners, in combination with pitons or slings secured to the rock, to protect the leader on a pitch.

Run-out The length of rope led by a leader between belays.

Sérac An ice tower on a glacier.

Slab A smooth rock face of varying angle (usually between thirty – seventy degrees).

Sling A short loop of rope – of varying length.

Stance A place, between pitches, at which the leader can rest and belay his second (or vice versa). Sometimes no suitable place can be found, and the stance has to be made in étriers.

Traverse A horizontal, or sometimes diagonal, movement over snow, ice or rock.

Verglas *(Fr.)* A thin coating of ice on rock.

Wall An extremely steep rock face. (Usually of more than seventy degrees.)

Wedges Usually wooden (latterly metal), and used in place of pitons in wider cracks.

PIZ MOLINO : North east face

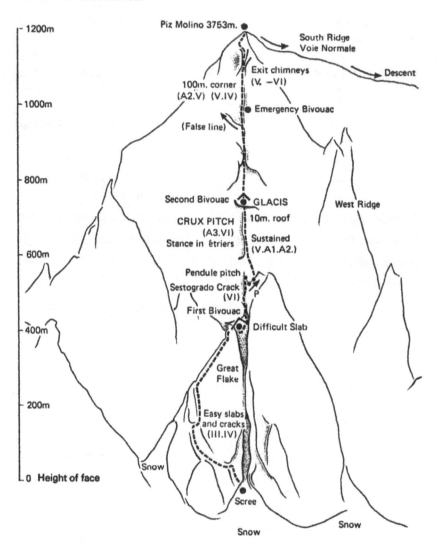

Piz Molino

Piz Molino: 3,753 metres

North-east face: Schiavi, Morra, T. Rinuccini, P. Rinuccini; August 1954, in three days.

Technical note: A great post-war climb done by a well-established team. At the time of writing it awaits a second ascent. The face is high (almost 1,200 metres) and, facing north, doesn't come into condition until late in the season. In some years the upper section (above the second bivouac) may never clear of ice. *There is some danger of stonefall.*

The line of ascent is always obvious. The pendule pitch marks a hiatus, as the main feature of the climb (the dièdre) closes for some seventy metres and the link with the upper dièdre is achieved by an airy swing across to a parallel flake crack. Once committed to the upper section it is probably wiser to press for the top rather than retreat down the face.

The bivouac at the top of the great flake is comfortable (ice patch for water). The second bivouac of the first ascensionists (in a cave at the back of the glacis immediately above the ten-metre roof) is safe and adequate but devoid of water.

Not all the pitons were left in place. Carry a good selection, especially of thin pitons for the 'sestogrado crack' (where the line closes). An ice axe and one pair of crampons may be useful. The rock is good. Diagram opposite.

Descent via south ridge (P.D: two and a half hours to Masino hut: cairns).

Start: 100 metres to right (north) of snow gully descending from east ridge, marked by characteristic tower on right below huge roof in centre of face. From scree gully follow obvious depression trending right to left for three rope lengths. Gain crest of arête and follow to breche overlooking smooth slab, and immediately below great flake at left of roof (III & IV: three to four hours); first bivouac.

Traverse right along ledge for ten metres (exposed). Climb slab below right edge of roof (VI: two pitons) to diagonal groove and traverse easily upward (right) to corner (good stance in dièdre). Climb chimneys above to gain access to central face. Follow dièdre to point where crack narrows. Stance below crack (étriers: two pitons). Climb with difficulty (VI: poor protection) the 'sestogrado' crack to high piton from which arrange rope and descend fifteen metres to make swing right and so gain footing on flake on right wall (piton in place: sling). Traverse up and left for seventy metres to re-enter dièdre (V+: two pitons). Climb straight to ten metre roof which closes groove. From stance (in étriers) surmount roof (hard: A3 & VI: danger of stonefall at lip) to small glacis. Second bivouac in cave below chimney.

Climb chimney (IV). Follow dièdre (three rope lengths: IV & V: pitons) to overhangs. A chimney splits the roof above. Climb it (at twenty metre stance: pitons). Climb chimney above (forty metres) to gain upper face (stance in étriers: two pitons). A groove bisects the steep slab. Climb it (hard: VI: pitons) to point where vague ramp leads left. *Do not follow this ramp* (piton left by Schiavi after false line taken). Continue straight up to reach clean-cut '100-metre' corner. Climb corner on pitons and by free climbing (strenuous), to reach exit chimneys (V- & IV) which widen out to summit ridge, and thus (easily) to top. The left-hand branch was taken on first ascent since the right-hand chimney held some large, loose blocks.

Part 1

1   Chapter 1

By noon they'd climbed more than 1,000 metres. At the head of the valley they turned to look back, but Molino was lost far below in the haze, where the river flashed briefly between the rocks.

Though they had travelled far from the village now, the most formidable part of the day's march still lay ahead. And when, at length, they plodded out of the forest and on to the stony rubbish of the terminal moraine, the small man recognised that landscape to which he never came, time after time, without a certain dread. Now he picked his way over the debris to where his companion sat, hunched and motionless, on a flat-topped rock beside the stream.

They were content to linger here by the stream. In the stillness of the amphitheatre the immensity of their undertaking seemed to loom menacingly above their heads. Later it would become a technical problem – something they would work upon together, like craftsmen working upon stone. But now, because they were tired, because they still had far to go, because the moment had not yet come, the north face thrust itself between them with a presence almost as tangible and as cold as the great buttresses which flanked its face.

For almost an hour they sat quietly by the stream. They had little to say to each other. The small man produced some lengths of stringy cabanos, and a hunk of cheese wrapped in grease-stained paper from the side pocket of his sac. They ate in silence. Occasionally his big, fair-haired companion got up and wandered among the boulders, staring up to where the final summit of the Piz Molino gleamed above the black granite cliffs of the amphitheatre.

'Not unlike the Cima Su Alto,' he said, at length.

The small man was groping with a greasy hand among the pebbles at the edge of the stream. The back of his hand was pitted and scarred. Its fingernails worn down. Grained with dirt.

'Didn't know you'd done it,' he said.

He took aim at a target on the far side of the stream.

'What?'

The pebble shot off a small red rock and bounced away.

'The Su Alto.'

'Winter ascent. With Belmonte.'

The big man sat down again on the flat rock, lay back and closed his eyes. He liked the sun.

'Yes,' he said. 'Six years ago on Christmas Eve. We bivouacked on the Gabriel-Livanos ledge.'

The other's arm paused in the act of throwing. The flaky, pale pink weal of a recent burn stood out against the brown edge of his hand. 'Christmas Eve!' His voice sounded incredulous.

'Jean-Louis had a few days off. And the conditions were right.'

The small man's pebble bounced again on the small red rock. His name was Daniel.

Christ! he thought. It wasn't a thing he'd have done himself – not on Christmas Eve – though it was typical of Belmonte.

'What was it like?' he asked, curiously.

'Bloody cold,' said his companion and sat up sharply.

Though the rock was warm he couldn't rest for long.

'We'd better get on with it,' he said.

They packed the remnants of their meal, hoisted the heavy sacs and made their way slowly, sweating already under the weight and heat, towards the ridge.

It was early when they had arrived that morning in Molino, the square silent. Empty. The sun was just getting up. They climbed down from the lorry, hoisting the big sacs with the slow engine rumble throbbing in their ears, shouting their thanks in bad German, and they saw no one. Only a young boy at the Albergo Montebello looked out of a bedroom window and saw them standing there in the first sunlight outside the Post, next to the poster that he liked (Daniel had noticed it: two white horses and a girl perched like a bird – CIRCUS ALBERTI, it said, in big curving letters, 13 AGOSTO 1965 – a year ago, exactly to the day).

Daniel was writing a postcard.

Dear Michel,

We are going to climb the big mountain in this picture. Then we shall come home. Look after Maman.

Love from
Papa

The great north face rose grandly above a pretty meadow filled with flowers. Daniel glanced at it briefly and dropped it in the box. The other card he looked at for a moment (addressed, stamped with a Swiss stamp, it bore no message), considered, and put it back into his sac. Then he saw the small face up at the window, above a box of red geraniums. He waved. The face vanished.

But the boy asked about them later. He asked the old man at the Post.

'There is only one reason why such men come to Molino,' the old man said, unfastening the shutter, nodding in the direction of the Val d'Averta – but the boy saw only the pleasant path past the dairy that led into the pine forest. Later that morning he set off along the path. Between the oaks and chestnut trees. Past the green banks of rhododendron, where the air was heavy with the scent of flowers and crushed grass and the piney smell of the forest. He did not get far. If he'd struggled on through the pine forest, he might have got up to the amphitheatre. But no further.

Even for the climbers it was strenuous. For three hours they struggled upward, stumbling over boulders, slipping on the steep wet banks of gullies, pushing through tangles of branches that struck back to lacerate their arms and faces. At one point the path steepened into a line of footholds traversing upward across an almost vertical wall, which they crossed swaying against the pull of the sacs. As the afternoon wore on the big man again drew further and further ahead. He bored on through gullies and streams, climbing higher and higher along the flanks of the ridge until he vanished from sight.

Daniel was glad to be alone. He was soaked with sweat. He felt sick. His breathing was beginning to hurt. The pack grew heavier. Eventually he could manage only a few yards at a time, staggering forward to whatever support might offer a few seconds' rest as he leant, arm rigid against tree or boulder, bent double under the pack. Gradually the tightness in his chest relaxed. He straightened again and plodded on.

He climbed slowly but steadily up between thinning clusters of pines, from darkness through shadow, and out at last into the sunlight. For a moment he stood motionless. Then he thrust the pack from his shoulders and ran forward through the grass until his boot caught against a stone and he fell heavily. He sprawled there in the warm grass and gazed and gazed on and on for 1,000 metres, up to the snowline and beyond it where the bare rock began, its buttresses, walls and pinnacles streaked by the snowfields and the hanging glaciers and the white, spidery fingers of the couloirs, all a far-off grey and deep shadowy blue, silent, empty of movement, under an empty sky. Far to the right in a deep cleft the snow glimmered between vast granite walls. Beneath it the glacier reared and twisted on its passage down to the valley. And beyond the glacier, flanked on either side by towering buttresses, loomed the enormous bulk of the north-east face. Of its features he could see nothing except the great Gothic arch of the summit soaring above the shadows of the north ridge. The rest was hidden in the gloom. But directly beneath the summit a thin, dark shade slanted down the grey expanse of the face. It was the 100-metre corner, the last barrier, over a thousand metres above the glacier.

In the spring that year, as he walked to mass one Sunday with the boy, he'd tried to pace out the configurations of that gigantic wall. At the end of the lane would be the first bivouac, with the roof above it, at 400 metres. Halfway across the field, the pendule – the rope-swing across the face. A hundred metres beyond it – where the footpath ran along the riverbank – the great roof. Then the second bivouac, then the corner, then the final chimneys. He didn't know about the summit. He wasn't sure he walked that far. For a black and white bird flew out of the hedge in front of them and then he was back in the familiar lane again, with the child tugging at his sleeve.

Now he looked up at the wall. He tried to think of his own countryside stretched out there. But they were not compatible. The imaginative effort was too much. Even with his eyes screwed tight it didn't work. Nothing would stay in place. The bridge collapsed. The river slid down over the field. Everything crumbled into a heap at the bottom of the face.

But it was time to move on. He got up from the grass and hoisted the heavy sac for the last time. Behind him the sun was sinking. The air seemed cooler. A few streaks of wispy cloud hung above the mountains. Cirrus, he thought it was called. He couldn't remember what it meant. Perhaps nothing. Above the deepening shadows on the wall the highest pinnacles of the north-east face were glowing a faint red. A great stillness brooded over the mountains; a silence broken only by the river roaring faintly in the valley a long way below. In this silence and stillness Daniel perceived the interminable cycles which had shaped this landscape. Suddenly he realised that they were never wholly still or silent. That they moved now, imperceptibly. That they would move for aeons after his death. That perhaps there was no final end to their task, no ultimate creation to which they aspired, for whatever they levelled in a million years, they might throw up again. And level again. He recognised that he, too, was as much their creature as the great wall which he had come to climb. For a moment he felt frightened and alone. The sun still shone on the green, empty meadow, on the jagged wall of rock that swept from end to end of the horizon. But he shivered a little. It was getting cold. Then, a little way below the hillock on which he stood, he saw the bright walls of a mountain tent pitched firmly within a ring of boulders. He saw its walls ripple slightly. The main guy quivered in the breeze. Through the entrance, in the dark orange gloom, he glimpsed the blue cover of a duvet. There was the big sac, its contents spilled out upon the grass: tins, bread, fresh fruit. And the stove was perched ready on a large flat stone. A moment later, the tall figure of his friend came up beyond the boulders, coming back with water from the stream.

2 Chapter 2

The next morning Daniel woke to the low clank of a sheep bell just beside his ear. The tent wall bulged dangerously. He scrambled out of his sleeping bag, unzipped the door and scuttled out, gesticulating ... The sheep skipped nervously away. Then turned, still chewing, to stare mistrustfully.

It was still early morning. A heavy dew had fallen. The wet grass curled around his feet, between his toes. It swept away in one unbroken, shimmering descent to the valley. He reached under the flysheet, and fished out the rest of the bread – it was stale anyway – and tossed it to the sheep. Then he went to make the coffee. In the ring of boulders about the tent there was a large granite table hollowed at its base and blackened by the fire they had made there the previous night. He placed the stove under the hollow, set the pan upon it and lit the gas.

I ought to write, he thought. Yet he remained squatting there by the stove, staring at the flame.

To leave like that, he thought. Coldly, with just a few curt words.

Within an hour of leaving he'd regretted it. Even as he got off the bus in Chamonix, stepping into the bright exciting world he loved, he felt ashamed.

I should write to her, he told himself.

He feared and hated quarrels. It was like the loss of grace to him. At first, whenever they parted on bad terms (in the early morning, perhaps, as he went to work) he would come back again the first chance he had. He did so in response to promptings, whether of guilt or pity, that seemed external to, and greater than, himself. He got up now and went back to the tent to get the biscuit tin in which he kept his pen and notebook. For three weeks he'd been trying to write; three weeks trying different phrases, different ways of saying things, striving for the right words to say what had to be said. Mostly not knowing what to say. In three weeks, moving from place to place (trying to write the letter), he'd sent over a dozen postcards. Each with a cheerful message, informing them that he was still safe and well, telling of little things he'd bought for the child. The squirrel badge from Cortina. The little doll on skis. And the carved wooden chamois which he held now, in his hand, as he searched in the big sac for the biscuit tin. He found it. Raymond was still asleep.

He crawled out of the tent again and crossed to the granite slab. He opened the tin and took out his passport, his wallet, some postcards, the badge he'd bought for the child and his pen and notebook. There, at the bottom, lay the envelope, clean and white, addressed already and stamped with a Swiss stamp. He wished he'd gone back again. But it would have done no good. She'd have said he'd come back so that he could go again and climb with an easy conscience. Perhaps that was true. Guilt made him mistrust himself.

He opened the notebook. The blank, white page confronted him. It was like a wall that kept out what had to be said, that turned his words back upon themselves. And he shrank back into silence – was kept there, unable to break out. Sometimes he was so defeated by the impossibility of saying anything that he was forced to retreat deep within his own borders, refusing to fight, holding himself back, striving not to feel, until this shrinking in upon himself contended with such resentment that he felt himself driven helplessly back towards resistance. And then he yearned to make a liberating gesture. Something decisive. A breakout that would be irrevocable. A scream of rage: a violent blow. Walking out altogether and never coming back.

He sat now on the granite slab, staring blankly at the notebook. The sun glared back at him from the empty page.

That wouldn't really change anything, he thought. It would be an evasion, a refusal to face the facts. Like a child storming away from the game he couldn't win, the pieces still there on the board. Still waiting a resolution. It would be like suicide. So he stayed, wishing it might be worth it.

In books or sermons, he thought, it's always worth it. And times of anger and isolation were like the hard moves that make a climb worthwhile, so that afterwards the bad moments seem a necessary part of it. Real life, he thought, is different. One stays because one has to.

The sheep bell clanked softly as the animal moved nearer the tent, cropping the short turf. Daniel stirred. He saw that he had written nothing.

But now the water was boiling fiercely. He climbed down from the slab and made the coffee. He put a great deal of sugar into one of the mugs, stirred it thoroughly, and carried it carefully over to the tent. Raymond was awake. He sat up, his knees hunched in the soft folds of his sleeping bag, and drank slowly, holding the mug with both hands close to his face.

After breakfast they sat outside the tent and sorted through the pile of equipment. The sun was rising higher in the sky. The circle of rocks around them shimmered with the first real heat of the day. Far off on the horizon the snowfields sparkled, and across the meadow, beyond the Zoccone spur, perhaps two kilometres away, the Piz Molino towered formidably above the glacier, its snow cone glittering in the pale blue sky.

The face was nearly 1,200 metres high. It was cold, dark and cheerless. And hidden for much of the day in the shadows of the ridges that flanked it on either side. Only in the early morning was it exposed to the sun. As the day wore on so the shadows crept back across the face. Even as they sat on the grass preparing their equipment the lower half of the face gradually dissolved in darkness once more. All around it, beneath the glacier and beyond the ridges, the sun glared from snow and ice and rock so that it was impossible for the eye to penetrate the dense blackness that draped the wall from ridge to ridge.

But the top of the face was clearly visible. Straight down the middle of it ran a thin line of shadow. It appeared shortly beneath the summit and vanished into the darkness 500 metres below. The north-east face was split by a huge dièdre – a corner shaped like an opened book which swept for almost a kilometre down the enormous wall. On either side of it the rock bulged forward, until the fault disappeared in a barrier of overhangs and projecting buttresses 300 metres or more above the glacier. From a small cave at the top of one of these buttresses, where the granite pillar joined the great face immediately below the dièdre, began the first pitch proper of the line the two men knew as the *direttissima* – the route they had come to climb.

Daniel had seen it first pictured in the pages of *La Montagne*. A huge, truncated pyramid of rock with the same dark shadow slanting down the face. A white dotted line had been superimposed upon the photograph. Underneath it, a caption.

LA VOIE DIRECTE AU GRAND DIÈDRE DE LA FACE
NORD-EST DU PIC MOLINO

Now, confronted for the first time by the face itself, he suddenly felt frightened. Not by the wall. Something else. He didn't know what it was.

But he was conscious, suddenly, of something that had happened long ago. He remembered the dark alcove under the stairs that led to the dormitory, the two rows of beds each with scarlet blanket and wooden locker; the dim, red glow of a single bulb; the shrouded cubicle; a sudden scrape of a curtain and (remembered for the first time in years but with the same clutching spasm) Brother Jerome. Every night he stood at the foot of his bed, holding himself very still, as Brother Jerome passed silently along the row of boys. Some of them kept a pair of clean underpants specially crumpled for his inspection. They never wore them. And Brother Jerome had never known. But he clutched his own soiled garment with fingers that trembled as the dark figure, its brass crucifix bumping softly against the black soutane, drew nearer. He must have been eight years old then.

And then, as he sat there sorting through the pitons and hollow steel wedges, it all came back in a flash: the refectory in Lent, the furtive, subdued clatter of plates and cutlery, and the great staircase where the light burned always before the statue of St Joseph. He'd never climbed it. No one had. God lived there, he used to think. And God was like Brother Superior. At Corpus Christi he used to walk gravely before the Blessed Sacrament, scattering petals on the gravelled paths. The white procession pacing slowly past lawns and tall banks of purple rhododendron. While the choir sang 'Lauda Sion Salvatorem'.

As he sat, a little dazed, absorbed in these fragments of his childhood, his fingers sorting mechanically through the pegs, he came back, again and again, to the image of Brother Jerome. Silent and black. Always black. Save for that cold edge of brass gleaming upon his breast.

All the delight Daniel felt in the bright air now left him. He felt flat and a little frightened, without knowing why. He looked out across the sunlight at the shadow beyond the glacier and shivered.

Christ knows what I'm doing here, he thought.

3 Chapter 3

Schiavi ... Giuseppe Mona ... the two Rinuccinis.

They would have crossed this meadow twelve years earlier on their way to this face. Ahead of them, three days on the wall. Three days to force the sestogrado crack, discover the pendule, find a route up roof and corner until Schiavi led them out on to the summit, exhausted, into a blizzard. As they started down the *voie normale* Piero Rinuccini collapsed and died. The blizzard thickened. The broad slope dissolved in front of them. The landscape blotted out. They sank up to their thighs. Schiavi drove on relentlessly far into the third night with the younger Rinuccini stumbling on in blind obedience. Until he, too, crumpled into the snow. He died less than 300 metres from the hut.

As he plodded towards the glacier Raymond's mind turned inevitably to the four Italians. He would have liked a few days' rest at the tent. They were tired – of climbing, of travelling, of carrying heavy sacs. But the weather never settled for long. The face attracted many storms. Stonefall and storms. They could not afford to wait. So he plodded on, stepping skilfully between the broken boulders, with his companion following doggedly behind.

In the remote pasture where the two men walked there was scarcely a sound. No noise of the river. Only grass swishing under foot. The muffled chink of steel. All around them the grass shimmered in the still air. Sometimes a faint tinkling of bells drifted upwards from the pine trees, where the sheep stirred spasmodically, cropping the turf at the edge of the forest. And Raymond plodded on, thinking of the Italians. Without alarm. But taking stock of all the possibilities. It was his custom to do so. The mountain was remote. Inaccessible. The face rarely in condition – except in a dry season. Parts of it were always verglassed. Always difficult. And the consequences of being caught by a storm on the upper section could be extremely serious. He would not court danger for its own sake. There were such men, but he was not one of them. He climbed mountains to earn his living, not to lose it (as some of his friends had lost theirs). He was a professional. Yet there were times when that profession was not enough, when he needed to go beyond the safer limits of the strictly necessary. Even then he refused to risk life wantonly and was contemptuous of those who did.

Courage and determination were not for him merely romantic ideals. They were necessary, like fear. If ever he was frightened it was because he felt himself no longer in control. And the solution was always the same. Either he restored control or he retreated. Stonefall, avalanche, bad weather, he could not control. So he feared them always and avoided them if he could. But the hard move he never feared. Some shrewd instinct, born of a long experience of difficulty, told him whether it would go or not. And if he thought a move would go, performing it was for him merely a technical problem. If it wouldn't go he left it alone. But there was always a possibility that chance might deprive him of his mastery of things. And that he feared. And since such a possibility was both a condition of his calling and a circumstance beyond his control he endured it stoically. On this occasion chance counted for more than he cared normally to accept. But he was well equipped. His ability beyond question. And Daniel a competent second. Raymond had a cautious faith in his power to survive all but the worst misfortune. Yet he kept a sharp eye on the weather.

He never climbed without protection. A few seasons earlier he'd had an object lesson in what happened to people who climbed without protection. A new route on the Triolet, with Sepp Böhlen, from Munich. Sharing the lead, pitch after pitch, for 200 metres. Then the greasy, overhanging corner. Böhlen embarked confidently, disappeared above the bulge while he remained below, wedged in the tiny stance, paying out the rope, waiting uneasily, waiting for the bang of a hammer.

It was an intimidating place. A bad place to hold a fall. But there was no sound of a hammer. Madman, he thought. The rope crept steadily upward. A few pebbles scattered down the corner.

Then, quite suddenly, a loud screech, the German dropping like a stone clear of the rock, the rope flying out, himself pulling it in desperately to check the fall, the flying coils tightening around Böhlen's thigh, poor Sepp screaming as the bone snapped. He'd stopped the fall. But he'd not forgotten. His hands took nearly a month to heal.

Now, at the height of his powers, his great strength directed by shrewd judgement, Raymond was very good (better, perhaps, than Schiavi at his prime). And he knew it. And sometimes, upon the great faces, the knowledge weighed heavily. He was a profoundly responsible man. After his brother's death on the Aiguille du Plan he'd wandered for weeks alone through the low woods and valleys of his home. Or forced himself up familiar routes, with perplexed clients wondering at the guide who scarcely spoke but took such care for their protection.

Gradually he came to accept that death as he had accepted the deaths of others. Bitterly, and without consent. He never considered abandoning his profession. He never questioned the validity of his work. Nor did he care to answer those who did. Though once, a long time ago in Chamonix, he'd spoken to a journalist.

'You write,' he said hesitantly, 'of our *conquering* mountains – as if we were the heroes of some preposterous war. It's not like that. What you call "victory", or "defeat", is meaningless. That we have survived again is the only victory. It is significant to us alone. There is nothing else.'

They came at last to a steep bank littered with boulders where the grass grew sparsely between heaps of rubble. They had reached the moraine. Below it the Vadrecc del Zoccone rolled past them like a grimy bandage. In summer the snow melted on the lower glacier. The ice was stained with puddles and scarred by the cracks of small crevasses. Patches of gravel and loose stones were scattered haphazardly, and a thin watery film covered the surface. Six hundred metres away a long spur from the Piz Zoccone curved down like a root into the medial moraine separating the main glacier from its tributary, the Vadrecc del Molino. Both were in retreat. The moraine was scattered for many yards on either side of the spur, and the deep ravine of the bergschrund below the rock had filled with rubbish. They descended cautiously through the debris and stepped out across the slippery ice, threading their way between the crevasses towards the ridge.

Even a dry, harmless glacier such as this was a strange place to be. Once it had filled the valley. Now, in its decline, it was retreating towards the snowfields, high in the mountains, which had been its source for nearly a million years. As they crossed the Zoccone glacier Daniel recognised that they had come to a place where time, as he understood it, was negligible. All the years of his entire life could count for scarcely more than a hundred feet in the imperceptible frozen journey that creaked and whispered all around him as the glacier shifted in its rocky bed. Such recognitions frightened him.

They came at last to the spur and climbed slowly over the easy slabs to the crest, twenty or thirty metres above the moraine. They paused for a few moments and looked down for the first time at the Molino glacier. Steep. Narrow. Heavily crevassed. The sun scarcely penetrated its enclosing walls. So the snow never melted here. It softened a little in the early morning, but towards midday, as the shadows lengthened over the glacier, it began to freeze again. They descended to a small shelf, just above the ice, where a bank of snow curled over the deep ravine of the bergschrund, within two or three metres of the rock. Here they took off the sacs, uncoiled the climbing rope and tied on to double lengths, half red, half white. Daniel waited while the leader secured the belay. These preparations always unsettled him.

'OK,' said Raymond.

Daniel took the ice axe in his right hand and a few coils of the doubled rope in his left, and leapt out, well clear of the bergschrund, on to the hard snow. He drove the ice axe deeply into the snow, well back from the lip, tied back his

own rope in a figure-of-eight knot, clipped it to the axe head, and then collected the sacs as they came swaying down from the shelf above his head.

His companion leaped the gap with practised ease.

Then they began a weary trudge up between the Zoccone spur and the long,
north ridge of the Piz Molino. Daniel carried coils of the doubled rope in his
left hand. He plodded on between crevasses which he couldn't see, following
securely in the steps of his companion who read glaciers as other men read
books. The shattered séracs stacked insecurely in the icefall, each depression in
the snow – he strove to miss nothing. They climbed steadily for nearly a thousand metres until the glacier swung in a wide curve past the north-east face
and swept up to its source in the great north-west couloir of the Piz Zoccone.

They halted at the very edge of the ice. They had come almost to the head of
the glacier. The high ridge of the Molino–Zoccone traverse in front of them
and the spur to the left reared abruptly for hundreds of metres above their
heads. Behind them they saw their own steps fading down the steep slope to
the valley. Across the bergschrund the twin buttresses of the north wall towered like gigantic pillars before the doors of a dark cathedral. Between these
columns a narrow tongue of debris twisted upwards into the shadows of a
huge cave. There was no sound. The air was silent and cold. They stood
motionless in the snow. And they were silent too, as men stand silently in a solemn place or in the presence of death, except that the strange presence that
confronted them was not death. Nor was it life, at least not as they knew life,
but rather an indestructible persistence of mighty shapes, forms which stood,
or moved with the years, or changed, but were not dissolved: a presence from
which, although it did not live as they lived, they yet drew life.

They crossed the bergschrund on a bridge of hard snow and started slowly
up the steep scree which choked the gully between the buttresses. As they
penetrated further into the mountain the rock closed in on either side, and
they passed from the cold light of the glacier into a gloom where the air was
thick with the dank, earthy taste of boulder clay. The stones slipped and
shifted continually under their feet. The noise clattered between the vast
walls, a clatter of harsh reverberations which flowed into each other until the
narrow way was filled with clashing sound. Gradually, as their eyes accustomed to the gloom, the outline of the great cave emerged as a thicker
concentration of the general darkness, while high above their heads the jutting overhangs of the lower face took shape vaguely in the upper shadows. At
the back of the gully a long diagonal groove curved upwards across the left
wall in a great loop towards the main face. At its base the groove opened out
into a steep triangular slab streaked with water and split by a number of thin
horizontal cracks. The two men halted by the slab. Raymond unclipped the
karabiners (the two steel snap-links by which the doubled rope was fastened
to his waist-loop) and lit a cigarette, while Daniel recoiled the rope, dropping

it on the scree in doubled loops of red and white until the free ends lay on top. He packed the demountable ice axe in the big sac and laid out the slings, the piton carrier, the two helmets and the big hammer. The leader stubbed his cigarette against the buttress. He picked up both ends of the rope, retied each to a separate karabiner and clipped them to his waist-loop. He hung the nylon slings and the oval piton carrier across his shoulder, pushed the hammer securely through the tab behind his hip pocket, fastened his helmet and turned to the slab. It was five o'clock in the afternoon.

He moved steadily upward, pausing only to force a steep bulge at the mouth of the groove. Behind him the red and white lines of the doubled rope flashed across the dark granite. Daniel stood in silence, his eyes fixed upon the groove. His hands moved rhythmically, plucking the coils and flipping them upwards, the rope sliding over his shoulder, across his back and out from under his left arm. He could hear somewhere the faint drip of water. His feet were cold. A few pebbles trickled down from the buttress as the rope stirred against the rock. The tips of his fingers were growing numb, but he watched the red and white ropes moving up the groove long after his friend had disappeared. And when the ropes stopped moving and a muffled shout came ringing down between the walls he hoisted the heavy sac on to his shoulders, kicked his boots against the rock and set off to join his companion.

The climbing wasn't hard. After a hundred metres or so the groove ran out below an overhanging wall and the two men traversed a thin line over steep slabs towards the front of the buttress. The landscape shrank steadily beneath them. The rock steepened. As the difficulty increased Daniel began to doubt whether they were on the right line. Schiavi's account of the buttress indicated no climbing harder than the fourth grade. The big sac dragged on the harder moves. Daniel grew flustered. Jumpy. He began to mutter under his breath.

'Hard for four,' he grumbled. 'Bloody hard for four.'

Raymond ignored him.

A long series of walls and corners brought them at last to a dead end under another overhang. They consulted together under the roof. The leader was in no mood to face an ignominious descent to the groove. A thin intermittent fracture in the right wall offered a possible alternative (to Daniel it looked appallingly exposed). Raymond inspected it, his fingers exploring every wrinkle in the granite. Cautiously, he stepped along the crack.

'It's all right,' he shouted, at the end of the traverse. 'It'll go.'

Yet he paused, reluctant to leave the wall. Secure on the tiny holds he could have stayed for ever. Poised, the immensity of air beneath him. But the doubled rope tugged at his back, as if to remind him. And he had not forgotten. He stepped up into the groove.

Daniel settled himself beneath the roof and prepared for a long, uncomfortable delay. He fed the doubled rope out across the wall. It hung motionless for minutes at a time. He heard the bang of the big hammer and the high-pitched wincing of pitons driven deep into the rock. He remembered their first climb together on the east face of the Grand Capucin.

'Never use one peg where six will do,' his friend had shouted down from the first of the big overhangs, then lay back against the pull of the ropes, body arched, legs straddled, thrusting the old-fashioned ladder-like aluminium étriers in opposite directions, and swung the big kilo hammer crashing into the roof. The steel pegs rang like bells over the Tacul glacier.

Daniel looked at his watch. The mistake had cost them nearly an hour. When the shout came he clipped the sac to a knot in the white rope and sent it swaying across the wall.

The traverse was hard and very exposed. Like traversing the very edge of space. But the white rope circled his body. He heard his friend's deep voice singing somewhere in the gloom overhead. He leant backwards happily to hammer out the pegs. It took him a long time to retrieve them, and at eight o'clock, when they climbed out upon a broad platform over 300 metres above the glacier, they were still some distance from the top of the buttress.

They stopped to rest for a few minutes. Raymond lit a cigarette and sat down wearily on the big sac. The sun was setting. The western flanks of the higher peaks glowed with a golden light that spread slowly over the grey rock. They could see the valley and the village beyond it and even the road winding through the Oberhalbstein and all of it reduced somehow, shrunken, like the surface of a pricked balloon.

'You get a different view of the world up here,' said Daniel suddenly.

The leader nodded. He could still hear the faint sound of sheep bells from the pasture near the forest. Somewhere in the valley, or on the slopes of the meadow, a dog barked. In the village the women were lighting lamps. A bus droned heavily up the hill from the Italian border. Everywhere men were returning home. He sat motionless on the sac, the cigarette smouldering in his hand, gazing down towards Molino, at the life he sensed flowing beyond the village, beyond the dark line of distant hills. But he said nothing. At last he stood up, crushing the cigarette beneath his boot.

'We'd better get on with it,' he said.

Just before nine o'clock they reached the top of the great flake which formed the summit of the buttress. It was almost dark. They could see nothing clearly. A flimsy haze hung like wood smoke in the valley. Above it, on either side, black ridges loomed. The river and the glacier below them gleamed faintly through the dusk, and beyond the horizon the last traces of colour were draining fast from the sky. They came down from the flake easily on to a broad platform protected by the huge overhang of the first roof. A few metres away to the right began the first pitch of the *direttissima*. The ledge was littered with small stones and there were several large patches of ice. It was a good bivouac.

Raymond cleared away the stones while his companion unpacked the big sac. They fixed the tent-sac to the wall with pitons. Daniel lit the stove. They ate their supper slowly and when it was finished they sat on the coiled ropes with their backs against the face and drank the good hot coffee.

They sat for a long time, smoking, staring out across the glacier. It was completely dark now, and very cold. Overhead the stars glittered. There was one in particular, hanging low in the sky, just above the dark, curving line of the horizon. Daniel gazed at it for several minutes. It fascinated him.

'How did it all start?' he asked. 'The stars and everything.'

The leader made no reply.

'You must have thought about it sometimes.'

Raymond shook his head.

'But you must have asked yourself how it all started,' Daniel insisted. 'Do you think it's always been there?' Raymond considered.

'No,' he said eventually. 'If it was always there … if there was always *something* there … then it must have come from somewhere. Nothing can exist of its own accord.'

'Perhaps there was a tremendous explosion,' said Daniel. 'That's one theory. There was this tremendous explosion and all the stars and planets were thrown out into space.'

Raymond considered this, too, in silence.

'No,' he said. 'To say there was nothing, and then BANG there's something, is absurd. Nothing can come from nothing.'

Daniel grinned.

'Perhaps God created it, after all,' he said.

He would have a lot to answer for, thought Raymond, if he did. But he said nothing, sitting impassively on his coil of rope, the cigarette smouldering in his hand. In the village the lights were going out. Only a, handful remained, burning steadily through the darkness.

For a long time after his companion had gone to sleep, Daniel sat alone on the ledge. He's different, he thought. Quite different from me.

At first he heard the sound of the river quite plainly but after a while it seemed to disappear. A few lights glimmered faintly from the village. All around him the mountain was frozen and silent. Profound stillness. For a long time he looked up at the stars. He watched the pinpricks of light that had travelled across unimaginable distances. From stars, worlds (whatever they were) that had been cold and dark for thousands upon millions of years. He thought of the light travelling past him, beyond the farthest limit of his galaxy, out into the uncreated future to illumine worlds that had still to be. Once, there was nothing. Not just emptiness, or space, nothing! Then … BANG – there's something! Or, say there was *always* something. Not just something for a very long time, but always something. Always! Impossible to think of. He remembered lying in the darkness of the long dormitory, dark but for the glow of the red bulb, a child, trying to think … to push out the barriers around his childish perception. But now, as then, the effort to hold on faltered and collapsed.

For a long time he sat huddled on the ledge, staring into the darkness. He felt tired. Intensely cold. He began to shiver. Sometimes he dozed but irregular, violent fits of shivering shook his body, and he woke uncertain of where he was, or of what he'd come to do. The cold advanced steadily. He realised, vaguely, that he must get into the tent. But once there, huddled in his duvet and short *pied d'elephant* close to the body of his companion, he shivered for a long time before slipping at length into a cold uneasy sleep. He dreamt. In his dream he looked down at two hooded figures lodged precariously beneath the crumbling buttresses of a great north face. One paced aimlessly up and down the ledge. The other crouched over a small stove and tried to shield it with his body against the driving rain. He poked at the contents of a blackened saucepan. Water trickled incessantly through the crevices of the overhanging rock above their heads. The wind beat at them. At intervals they argued bitterly, their arms flapping in angry gestures.

Then he woke, sweating with panic, staring into the darkness. And realised he was trapped. Held here between earth and heaven, with no way of escape.

After that, fear kept him awake. At one o'clock he closed his eyes and made a last effort to ward off the nightmare reforming silently in the darkness all around him. He cast his mind out desperately towards secure, familiar objects: his companion, the outline of the tent, anything. And it came to rest, thankfully, in the image of his own child, sleeping quietly, across the frontier in another country.

4 Chapter 4

That year the child's birthday came on Easter Monday. He wore the blue coat Aunt Catharine had given him. He wore his shiny rubber boots because of the mud. At first he held his mother's hand, but at the first sound of the fair he tore loose and ran across the field. His boots made a little drumming sound in the grass. When she called his name he ran back towards her, almost tripping at her feet. Then off again, running with immense effort. Head thrown back, short arms thrusting like shuttles. When he saw the white horses under the coloured lights he cried, 'Dada! Dada!' and ran on to see them rising and falling, rising and falling, on the slowly turning roundabout. He couldn't reach the stirrups, but clung to the pole, face glowing, both legs pressed tight against the carved white sides. He called to them. She smiled back and waved her hand. Then the music started. He and the horse rose slowly as the roundabout began to turn. And she prepared to wave. The music blared, the horses flew around and all the children shrieked and waved.

But he spun by, clinging in terror to the leaping pole.

She waved and shouted. Uselessly.

The panic-stricken face flashed past again. If it screamed no one noticed. The blurred face whirled round with the blue coat and the poles and horses. At last the fairground man stepped to the centre of the roundabout and switched off the motor. Then stepped back again and held the child tightly until the spinning stopped. He was very upset.

It wasn't his fault, Daniel told him. It was no one's fault. He lifted the little boy from the wooden horse (how those arms had clung to him convulsively) and folded his arms around the small, shuddering body.

It was then he heard the voices.

At first he paid no attention. Then it occurred to him that the voices had no business to be heard on the north face. He scrambled out and up to the lip of the flake and strained to listen. Nothing – except the noise of the wind. Then he heard it again. Two voices. A long way off. Calling to one another. He wondered if it might be workers at the forestry site in the valley. Sounds carry a long way in the mountains. Then the sharp CRACK CRACK of a hammer. He heard it again, the repeated CRACK CRACK CRACK of a hammer flowing out over the wall. That settled it. He slid down from the flake and rushed back to the tent.

'There's someone on the face,' he said.

Raymond stared at him in disbelief.

'I've just heard their hammer.'

Raymond scrambled out of the tent.

'Might be on one of the ridge routes –' he began.

'No! They're on the face. I told you, I heard their hammer. They're some-where below the flake.'

'Christ! That's just about all we need. That'll screw everything up.'

But Daniel had climbed back to the top of the flake. He leant in against the easy-angled slab and peered over the edge.

'Two of them,' he said. 'They're below the big ledge. It'll take them a good hour to get here.'

'Right!' said Raymond. 'Let's get on with it.'

He hated chance encounters of this kind. Usually it meant delay. Either they held you up or you held them up. Either way it was bad for the nerves. If any-thing went wrong you had to help them (and the more people on a hard route the greater the chance of something going wrong). It might even mean com-petition. Racing to stay in front. He shook his head in disgust.

'Look,' he said. 'You get something to eat. I'll pack the gear.'

He wanted to be on the difficult slab before they arrived. He began to clear the tent while Daniel busied himself with bread, butter, biscuits and a large tube of honey. They worked quickly. All the time the banging and shouting grew louder. The climbers were evidently in high spirits and they moved fast, much faster than Daniel had anticipated. Before they'd finished their breakfast there was a loud, triumphant shout at the very edge of the flake. Raymond shrugged disgustedly. But Daniel went forward to greet the stranger.

He was a very big man, and he wore a faded blue duvet that was too small for him. The padded jacket, stretched tightly across the chest, made him look enormous. He had a broad, red face with immensely thick eyebrows almost joined together, and a scarlet woollen hat pulled down over his forehead. He stood for a moment at the very edge of the flake, staring in surprise. Then he turned, shouted excitedly at his unseen companion, gathered the rope with his left hand and leaped down the slab. He spoke briefly and stretched out his arm with a broad smile. Daniel shook his hand. The stranger spoke again, enquir-ingly, in the same deep, unintelligible tongue. Then, when Daniel smiled and shook his head, the stranger prodded himself in the chest with an emphatic finger.

'Tomas!' he said.

He spoke very deliberately, extending the syllables as if he were addressing a small child.

'Tomas!' he repeated. Then, waving an arm vaguely over the glacier, 'Jaro!'

'Jaro!' repeated Daniel.

He was glad they'd come. Their voices ringing up and down the rock dispelled the silence that hung about the face. Now everything was restored to life again. Although the sun had gone from the wall, it shone on the lower peaks across the glacier, and the bright light spread like a tide over the meadow. By the forest the sheep were stirring again. He heard the faint sound of their bells – then a fierce voice, shouting, just below the flake. An armful of loose coils swung over the top of the rock.

'Jaro?' asked Daniel, smiling.

'Jaro!' agreed the giant.

The newcomer was a squat, powerful man with a dark beard. He wore a scruffy, red cagoule tied at the waist with cord, and a fine white cap of a kind popular with the guides of the Oberland. He shuffled down from the flake and stood beside his friend, peering suspiciously from under the wide brim of his cap.

Silence.

The two strangers stood uncertainly, one anxious and smiling, the other defiant, doubtful of the outcome of this encounter, like men who might have welcomed a gesture of friendship but didn't expect it.

'Coffee?' asked Daniel.

They understood that. The giant beamed and Jaro expressed his thanks in one sombre syllable.

Daniel led them down to the bivouac.

'I'm going to make some more coffee,' he said.

Raymond said nothing. But Daniel knew very well what he was thinking, as he sat impassively on the coiled rope, sorting through the equipment. The big sac was almost full and only the cooking gear and a few scraps of food remained to be packed.

'I'm going to make some more coffee,' he repeated. Raymond looked up. He stared for a moment at the strangers but he didn't speak to them. He picked up the torn packet of Celtique from the ledge, took out a cigarette, and replaced the packet carefully in his breast pocket.

Hurriedly the giant fumbled for something. He found it, bent down, and offered a shiny, new Feudor to Raymond who reached up to take it. He flicked it. It didn't work. He flicked it again several times, pausing fractionally between each attempt. Eventually a tiny flame jumped and hovered precariously above the nozzle. He lit his cigarette, handed back the lighter and nodded his thanks. Then bent down again to his work.

Daniel wanted to explain that his friend was a good man and a fine climber. But he didn't know the words. And the coffee wasn't ready. He picked up the tattered packet of biscuits and held it out to the strangers.

'Biscotto,' he tried. Then, in German, *Keks?*'

He took the tube of honey and offered that as well. They stared at him blankly.

'Honey,' he said.

Since he couldn't remember 'honey' in any other language but his own he buzzed at them like a bee, bobbing his head and flapping his arms ridiculously. Still the giant didn't understand. He muttered a few uncertain words to Jaro who replied firmly, in deep decisive tones. He accepted the biscuits and the tube of honey and stood awkwardly, holding one in each hand.

'Danke! ' he said. 'Danke schön.'

Daniel sat down by the stove and spooned coffee into the mugs.

'Where are you from ?' he asked. 'What is your nationality?'

Then he remembered to put it into German.

'Welche Staatsan,' he began to stumble.

No response.

He tried again, with different words.

'Aus Welchem Lande kommen Sie?'

'Welchem Lande?' repeated Jaro – he didn't really understand.

'Nationalitlät?' said Daniel.

'Ah!' said Jaro, suddenly understanding. 'Wir sind Tschechen.'

'Ah!' said Daniel. 'Prague! A beautiful city! Praha – eine schöne Stadt.'

Then he remembered he'd never been to Prague, never seen it, even in pictures. Feeling ridiculous he turned aside to see to the coffee. As they sat down together to drink it Raymond came over and sat beside them.

'They're Czechs,' said Daniel.

Raymond nodded. The giant produced a bar of chocolate from his pocket and broke it into four pieces.

'Schweizer,' he said. 'Sehr gut!' He handed it round.

Raymond had not changed his mind. He regretted their coming. Nevertheless, he felt compelled to take a part in this exchange of courtesies. He sensed the tenuous alliance growing between the others, recognised the clumsy solicitude with which each man strove to sustain it as an attempt to establish life in one of the most inhuman places on earth. It was like carrying a stretcher, or pulling a rope, or shielding a flame that might otherwise go out. It called for one's support. So he supported it, in spite of himself. When the giant showed an interest in his helmet, he picked it up and held it out (the buckle, he saw, was really very loose: he'd noticed it the day before).

'Very strong,' he said.

He imitated the high-pitched whistle of falling stones, then, lifting his fist, crashed it down on top of the helmet. The giant understood. He pulled off his own scarlet woollen hat and shook it disparagingly.

'Nicht sehr gut,' he said.

But he, too, noticed the loose buckle. Tapped it with his finger.

'Needs fixing,' Raymond agreed, and thought to ask Daniel if he'd brought the needle (yes, he'd brought it – he always brought everything – it was in the little flat biscuit tin).

'Do you want to do it now?' Daniel asked, at the end of their meal. He was packing the last bits of equipment into the big sac.

But Raymond had gone off with the Czechs to the far end of the ledge and was now staring up at the rock. The upper face was hidden above the massive overhangs of the first roof. It thrust out from the steep slab on either side of him as far as he could see. In the centre it curved upwards like a Gothic arch. Here at the apex of the slab, seventy metres above the ledge, the great roof was split by a deep chimney. It offered a narrow passage to the central section of the face.

The first pitch was of the sixth, and hardest, grade. The slab was of light grey granite, very steep and smooth, and lacking any crack or groove that might offer a plain route to the roof. Three convex bands, one above the other, ran prominently across the rock. There was nothing else. Raymond looked at the slab for a long time. He recalled the terse phrases of the article in *Alpinismus*: a thirty metre run-out – one peg beneath each of the first two bands nothing else. According to Schiavi there was no protection on the last band, the crux, at twenty-five metres. But the rock was dry. No ice (as far as he could see). No danger of stonefall. It was a pure rock pitch, harmless, though very severe. At last he found what he was looking for. He saw, six or seven metres up the slab, the rusty head of an old piton sticking out under the first band. He couldn't see anything under the second band. It was too far up. But he knew, now, where the line went.

'One might as well begin with a pitch of six,' he said.

'Can't get any harder,' said Daniel.

'Oh, yes!' said Raymond. 'It can always get harder.'

He fastened his helmet (it was still loose) while Daniel tied on to the double rope. He laid out the coils, loop by loop, and handed the free ends to the leader.

'*Viel Glück!*' the giant called out.

Raymond nodded. Turned to the slab.

He made two mantelshelves, one after the other, hoisting himself on small striations barely wide enough for the fingers of one hand. The second was particularly hard. There were no holds above the mantelshelf, and he inched his body up against the friction of the slab until he stood straight on the tiny ledge. Now the first band reared up from the rock no more than a metre above his head. He could see the peg plainly, lodged in a lateral crack on the underside of the bulge. He stretched his left arm as far as he dared without shifting the delicate balance of his body. He couldn't reach it. He tried again, this time with his right arm, searching the bottom of the band until his fingers came up against a narrow undercut. He pulled strongly against the sharp edge and brought both feet higher up the slab, leaning backwards on his right arm. He reached again for the peg and grasped it. It came out. Immediately he swung off balance, dropping the peg, pivoting out of control around the hold. Only a swift jab sideways with the right foot fended off the fall. The three men below watched in silence.

But if Raymond was startled by the incident he didn't show it. He leaned forward slightly, supporting himself against the rock with his forearm, and groped for the piton carrier. He chose a thin leaf-bladed peg, pulled out the big hammer (it was slung on a cord from his waist), and climbed up to the band. He slotted the peg into the crack and drove it home left-handed. Then he came down again to the ledge. His left leg was trembling, and he found it increasingly difficult to stand in balance on the tiny hold. He fastened two snap-links on to the alloy karabiner, clipped one to the étrier, the other to the red rope and took hold once more of the undercut. The fingers of his right hand ached abominably. The pain seemed to run on wires along his forearm and up into the shoulder. He clipped the karabiner to the peg and grasped it.

'Red,' he shouted.

Daniel leant backwards, tightening the red rope with the full weight of his body, and Raymond stepped across into the étrier.

'Schwer!' said the giant.

Daniel grinned. Nodded.

But his eyes never left the figure flowing up the steep, smooth slab, pulling out over the bulge of the second band ('white rope!' it shouted), going up, it seemed, like the lark in the song. It reminded him. Something about a swimmer? Somebody's spirit like a swimmer? Yes! Furrowing happily across.

'L'im-men-si-té pro-fon-de!'

He remembered the heads turning towards him, monsieur's blunt finger stabbing out the syllables.

'What does it mean – "l'immensité profonde" ?'

It means, monsieur, among other things, the north-east face of the Piz Molino. He would have liked to have said that.

'Bitte?'

It was Jaro. He'd gone along the ledge to his sac and come back with his camera.

Daniel grinned.

'They want to take a picture,' he shouted.

Raymond looked down from under the third band. 'Never mind the pictures,' he shouted. 'You watch the bloody rope.'

'Go on,' said Daniel to Jaro.

'How's it going?' he shouted.

But Raymond didn't answer. He had reached the crux. The third band was much more formidable than the first two. It stuck up from the rock like a chimney stack from a roof. Except that the slab was steeper than any roof. At its base it overhung slightly, offering a flat edge to the hand. This, and a small flake halfway up, was all that he could see. Beyond that, the rock curved back out of sight.

He remembered that Schiavi had found no protection here. But it was twelve years since the Italians had climbed this slab. He searched carefully but could find nothing that would take a peg. He noticed a small, round protuberance in the granite. Too far to one side to be of any use as a hold. There was a hairline crack on its upper slope. He leant into the slab slightly, resting on his forearm, took the hammer and chipped speculatively at the crack. It lengthened a little. He chipped at it again, gently, until he had picked out a narrow channel where it joined the rock. He took one of the thin wire slings from his shoulder and hung it over the bump, pushing it down into the crack and weighting it with two heavy karabiners. It wasn't much. But it would do for the move.

He clipped in the white rope and pulled out an arm's length of slack. Then he tried to work it out. Although he could reach it, the bottom edge of the band was still too far above him. He needed to get much closer. If he could get the upper half of his body above it, he could use the edge as a hold. He could push down against the slab with his feet and pull upwards against the edge as if he were lifting it. It would be very strenuous, but it would hold him in position long enough to go for the flake. It was really a simple mechanical problem.

But, as far as he could see, there were no holds that would get him up to the band. And even if he got there the convex curve would force him out beyond the vertical. He knew that if his body was pushed beyond a certain point the mechanics wouldn't work. He'd just fall backwards down the slab. And it was a blind move. Even if he got as far as the flake he didn't know what lay above it. There must be something there. Schiavi had climbed it (but that was twelve years ago, and he was not inclined to believe in the existence of holds he couldn't see and handle). But he was ten metres above the last peg. And the little wire 'runner' offered a very dubious protection. If he came off, and the 'runner' failed, he would fall almost twenty metres before he came to the peg.

But the real problem (he did not expect to come off) was to get up to the flake. If he got there – then found that the hold did not exist … He thought his chances of reversing the move were probably sufficient. He was fairly confident of that. He decided on a swift advance up the slab, trusting his speed and the friction of the granite to get him up to the band.

He made three short strides and caught the flat edge sharply with both hands just below the level of his right knee. But the curve was steeper than he thought. He was forced backwards – felt his fingers slipping from the edge. Instantaneously he went for the flake – found it with his right hand – and swung out from under the bulge. For a fraction of a second he hung clear of the rock as he struggled to get his left hand up to the flake. He had misjudged the curve completely.

On the ledge, twenty-five metres below, the three men watched tensely as the leader committed himself to the critical move. Each of them, at some time, had suffered the same few seconds of extremity. Daniel took a firm stance and prepared himself for an upward strain as Raymond hauled head and shoulders up to the flake, turned one hand sideways on the hold, and began the desperate press downward to raise the lower half of his body. He heard a flat clattering noise (it was the karabiner hitting the slab below him) and he knew that the 'runner' had come off. But his arm straightened slowly – his waist came up to the flake – he reached for the top of the band. He found a shallow crack a full arm's length above his head. It was all he needed.

'He's there,' said Daniel loudly.

Raymond climbed swiftly up the last few metres of the pitch. Where the slab and roof met, almost at a right angle, there was a deep fracture, like a shelf, running the whole width of the slab. He placed two pegs, one above the other, at the back of the shelf and clipped in his belay sling, fastening his étriers to the lower peg. Then he sat quietly on the slab with his feet in the étriers and lit a cigarette. It was cold and dark under the roof. But all the country below was lit by sunlight. He could see the mountains gleaming grey and white across the valley, beyond the Zoccone spur. And the glacier, and the forest, and the meadows and even the river, and all of it still and shining.

Nothing moved. Even the noises were distant and muffled. Like the wind that brushed against his face. Sitting on the slab, over 400 metres above the glacier, seeing everything spread out below him, he felt as if he were looking out from a secret place upon an unsuspecting world. The stillness and the great distance and the difficulties which now lay behind him contributed to his tranquillity.

I have come from down there, he thought. After all these years, it still seemed remarkable.

He stubbed out the cigarette and took in both ropes until they were tight. He tied back the white rope to one of the karabiners. The red one he lifted over his shoulder.

'Come on!' he shouted. 'Use the white – leave the pegs for the others.'

The Czechs were sitting on the ledge, gazing out over the valley, talking quietly in their own language. They looked up when Daniel spoke to them. They didn't understand. He made a loop in his own rope and held it out to them.

'You want it?' he asked.

The giant smiled and shook his head.

'*Nein, danke,*' he said.

Daniel shrugged. It was their affair.

'Well!' he said. '*Auf Wiedersehen!*'

The giant raised a hand.

'*Auf Wiedersehen!*'

'*Viel Glück!*' called out Jaro.

Daniel made no attempt to climb the slab properly. It was his business to bring up the big sac as quickly as he could. He was carrying most of the leader's gear as well as his own and even with a fixed rope he found the pitch difficult. He pulled himself up the white rope gathering the étrier, the sling and the karabiners as he came up to them. It was simple, brutal climbing, which, normally, he loathed. It was not dignified. But for once he found the rough work exhilarating. They were going well, in good weather, and there were no more than four pitches of six on the entire route. He found it impossible to repeat Raymond's manoeuvre at the crux so he tied an overhand knot in the white rope, stepped into the loop and hauled himself up and over the band.

'All right?'

'Not too bad.'

He clipped his sling and his two étriers to the karabiner in the upper peg. Then he sat down on the slab and kicked his boots between the rungs.

'Smoke?'

The small man took the half-smoked Celtique and put it between his lips.

'Right then!' said Raymond.

'Right! Be careful.'

'Always,' said Raymond.

Daniel watched him go, stepping crab-wise across the slab, his hands criss-crossing in the deep crack. Every few metres he paused to test the old pegs, tapping them with the big hammer, clipping in the ropes, first the red, then the white. Daniel sat gathering in the slack which hung down over the slab in two great loops. He slid the ropes around his body and passed them out along the traverse. When the cigarette was finished he took it awkwardly in his gloved hand and crushed it against the rock. He was not impressed by the view. He scarcely noticed it. But he gazed steadily at the blue duvet receding in the general darkness of the roof, towards the dark corner almost a rope's length away. When the call came he unclipped his sling, cleared his gear from the stance and set off along the traverse.

It began gently. There were plenty of holds in the deep crack, and he climbed easily across the angle of the slab, following the upward curve of the roof. He heard his friend singing softly in the dark corner. Down below the Czechs were on the move. He wondered how the giant would fare on the hard moves. He caught fragments of laughter. Deep voices drifted up on the wind.

'Hallo, Tomas!' he called.

He waited for the answering shout, indistinct, unintelligible, but there somewhere below the long sweep of the slab.

He moved on steadily, unclipping the ropes, collecting the karabiners. As he climbed further up into the recesses of the roof he passed small patches of ice. Pockets of earth scattered in the crack. Then a tiny plant with spiky, pink flowers growing precariously on the very lip of the shelf. Here, the roof tilted sharply. The crack narrowed to a few millimetres. He was almost at the centre of the lower face. At this point the slab immediately below him fell steeply into the great main wall which rose straight from the cave nearly 450 metres below. At its top right-hand edge the slab was bounded by a short wall, like a vertical buttress supporting the roof. In the very corner of this junction the leader sat in étriers eating a bar of chocolate.

'You'll need étriers for the last few metres,' he said.

He wedged his chocolate in a small fissure and tightened the ropes as his second reached for the next peg.

'That plant,' he gasped, as he stepped up into the étrier, 'in the crack … '

'Houseleek,' said Raymond.

Daniel climbed up to the top rungs of the étriers. The big sac dragged awkwardly in the corner. It was hard work.

'How did it get there?'

'How did what get where?'

'That plant.'

'Bird. Or the wind.'

The pegs seemed a long way apart to Daniel. He had to climb to the top rung of each ether, bend sideways to hold on to the karabiner, then stretch for the next peg.

'Do you think … it'll survive?'

'What?'

'That plant.'

'Who knows? It might.'

Only one peg between them now.

'You'd better belay me from there,' said Raymond.

He took the half-eaten bar of chocolate out of the fissure and tossed it down. Daniel caught it with one hand and put it between his teeth. He reached for the small hammer at his hip, drove a peg into the crack and secured himself to it with a short sling. He placed another peg beside the first and passed both ropes through the karabiner so that the pull, if it came at all, would fall directly upon the peg. Then he arranged himself in the étriers, tightened the sling securing him to the belay peg, turned sideways and took up both ropes at chest level. He ate the chocolate while Raymond prepared himself for the next pitch.

'Leave just the old pegs,' he said.

'Right. Where to now?'

'OK,' said Raymond.

He crossed the short wall on one peg and passed out of sight.

It was an awkward stance for Daniel. Uncomfortable. He sat with his boots pressed against the wall leaning backwards against the tight sling, staring at the peg which held it. He'd no idea where Raymond was. Occasionally he felt a sharp pull on one of the ropes as it was tugged up through the karabiner. From time to time he eased his buttocks to relieve the pressure of the rungs. Each time he saw the sling move, and the karabiner twist slightly in the peg.

If you stared at it long enough you could convince yourself that the peg was coming out.

He remembered the old guardian at the Cabane des Planches who used to warn everyone of the dangers of roping down without protection. It was his obsession.

'Tu sais, vieux, que tour les grands chefs se sont tués en rappel.'

Gaston used to mumble that to everyone.

And everyone laughed.

'When you were young, Gaston,' they said, 'the mountains were much bigger.'

But it had happened to Daniel once. On the big limestone cliffs of Vercors. On a long rappel from a wooden wedge. He could have been killed. He remembered how the wedge jumped suddenly in the crack. At first he didn't believe it. Couldn't accept it was happening to him. He relaxed his grip on the ropes – stepped down again.

The wedge tilted sharply.

Christ! It's coming out!

He stopped dead against the rock and whipped the ropes around the descendeur to check the descent.

He hung there a long time. Didn't dare to move. Didn't know what to do. It began to hurt. First a dull ache spreading across his back. Then a sharpening pain as the thin harness cut into his thigh.

He shouted.

No one answered.

He heard the drone of cars passing on the road. Nothing else had changed. He thought of Gervasutti – 'le grand chef' – climbing back to free a jammed rope. Suddenly the ropes collapsed on top of him. The white stone flashed past – then streaks of blue and vivid green across the valley – then the road – then the trees – then, as the limestone crag spun round again, he crashed backwards through branches and the spinning stopped.

Now, it amused him to think about it. The catastrophes one has survived become things to joke about. Sometimes he'd stare until he'd almost convinced himself that the peg was coming out. Then he would exert his will. Like a hammer. And drive it home.

Survival, he thought, is all that really matters.

5 Chapter 5

Raymond was in high spirits. It was still early, the weather fine. He perched like a bird on a narrow gutter above the chimney through which they'd climbed to reach the central section of the face. He had nailed everything to the rock. The ropes hung in neat loops over the rock. Now he sat eating rye bread and sausage, which he sliced against his thumb with a: horn-handled knife, peering down into the depths of the chimney. He was much amused by what he saw between his boots.

'Hey, Tomas!' he shouted. 'No room here. You'll have to stay where you are till I've had my breakfast.'

The giant paused for a moment and looked up wearily at the pair of boots that blocked the exit above his head.

'Tell him!' said Raymond.

He looked expectantly at Daniel who shook his head. Raymond bent over the space between his feet.

'No room here,' he shouted. '*Oben alles voll!*'

He passed the coffee across the gap.

'Here!' he said.

Daniel shook his head. The exhilaration he had felt in the sheltered climbing below the overhang had evaporated leaving a dry residue of fear. An hour earlier that fear stopped short at the first overhang. But now the real extent of their commitment climbed to its proper height upon the starkest wall he'd ever seen. It began here, at his left hip, and stopped at the great roof, 300 metres vertically above his head. Between him and the roof lay the sestogrado crack, the pendule, the return traverse, and nothing (whatever he did, wherever he turned his mind) could relieve the staggering exposure.

At that moment a head in a red, woollen hat rose out of the rock beneath his feet.

'*Allez la France!*' it said.

Perhaps it was the only French that Tomas knew. Raymond burst out laughing at the beaming face between his boots. Then bent to hoist the giant to a seat on the edge of the chimney.

'Up you come!' he said. 'Have my place. See if you can cheer him up.'

He jerked his thumb towards his second.

'*Er ist sehr.*' He couldn't think of the words. 'He thinks we're all going to fall off.'

'*Bitte?*'

Raymond grinned and shook his head.

There were good reasons for his high spirits. The route now followed an unbroken line almost to the summit. Here, for the moment, the climbing was steep, but relatively easy. The rock was clean and free of ice at the surface. He thought of what it would be like with verglas in the crack, with real ice all the way up, and was grateful for the good weather. It was bound to hold long enough to get them over the roof. The fault was wide and jagged, like the chimney below it. Narrower, but just as solid, with plenty of holds. Six to seven hours, he thought, depending on the pegs. That's all I need. After that there was only the corner.

He felt very confident. One more bivouac. The Masino hut tomorrow. Then it's over. Nothing but the most disastrous luck could stop him. Unless the weather broke a couple of hours before dawn. That would be bad. To be caught by storms on the upper face; to be up there, committed, in bad weather. But they were well equipped. The Czechs were evidently competent. His own second would do what had to be done. Then, for an instant, he remembered the terrible storm on the Plan. He shook his head. The storms here, he told himself, don't last as long as that.

Twenty metres up the dièdre he found the first piton. It almost fell out at the touch. He removed it. Italian. A thin-bladed Cassin, badly corroded. He noticed the initials stamped on the head. 'P.R.' It was Rinuccini's peg. It had been there for twelve years. He stared at the thing for a moment, wondering what to do with it. It didn't trouble him. He'd seen grimmer evidence on other mountains. But it was something they could do without.

'What's up?' shouted Daniel.

Raymond shook his head. He unbuttoned his thigh pocket and slipped the peg inside. Then he hammered in a new one, clipped in the red rope, and moved up. He climbed swiftly, pausing now and then to look up the long channel of the dièdre. He couldn't see much. The bulging walls on either side cut off most of the face. But he could see the roof, hanging like an enormous canopy. Still a long way off. He climbed with hands jammed in the crack, his feet straddling the gap from wall to wall, lifting his body steadily on small holds in the granite. It was called 'bridging', and he did it with great skill. He could climb even an overhanging dièdre with very little effort, as long as the walls were wide enough for him to stand vertically. He used to tell all the novices that.

'Attention!' he would say. 'Stand straight! Climb with the legs!'

He ran out almost a full rope's length until he had reached a point where the walls of the dièdre flattened suddenly. Here he rested. It wasn't possible to stand unaided. He placed the pegs and étriers and sat between the rungs with his boots on the sloping shoulder of rock. He could see much better now. Evidently he had reached the critical section. Above him the dièdre changed character. The rock rose almost vertically, protruding very slightly on either side of the crack which ran upwards, like a narrow gutter, for several hundred metres, then curved out of sight beneath the great roof.

He kept the rope tight while his second climbed and thought about the wall. He was impressed. Impressed, that is, as far as he would permit himself to be impressed by anything. Daniel imagined lightning striking the wall, or heard avalanches thundering down some terrifying couloir at the slightest provocation. But Raymond, who had endured these things, considered them as if they were no more than hazards in a textbook. If, as he always maintained, he had never climbed anything he could not reverse, it was because of this habitual assessment of possibilities. He took nothing for granted, invariably assumed the worst, and considered every means of avoiding its consequences.

Despite all opinions to the contrary he knew that in a crisis it was almost always better to retreat. On the upper face, above the roof, they would be exposed to the full force of any storm that struck the mountain. It was said that the route was irreversible. That above the pendule one was committed. He did not believe it. But a forced descent of the central wall would be a formidable task to which bad weather would bring immense difficulty and danger. The great roof – one of the biggest in the Alps – would have to be reversed. And below the roof, as far as he could see, there was nothing that could offer the smallest shelter on the long retreat. Each new descent would have to be made from étriers. Roping down was always hazardous. Many of the best men died that way. It was something he tried to impress upon the young men who came to him for instruction.

But he did not teach well. He had no talent for it. In the lecture room of the École des Hautes Montagnes he persistently reduced the experience of twenty years to a handful of propositions (for the most part commonplace paradoxes) which sounded trite in every ear but his own.

'All climbs end where they begin,' he would say. Or, 'The ascent is not concluded until one has descended safely.'

Whether such aphorisms were a crude simplification or the quintessence of his craft no one ever knew. But at night, in the Café des Nations, the novices mocked him, offering each other absurd advice across the wine-soaked tables.

'*Attention! Montez sur la tête,*' they said. '*Prenez conscience! Pensez, pensez avec les jambes!*'

And the older men would smile, remembering his formidable reputation.

He was not a popular man. After the Plan disaster, as the news swept through the bars and restaurants, they said of him, 'Ah! He has a genius for survival, that one!'

He knew nothing of this. But had someone told him of it he would not have been surprised.

'In the valley,' he would have said, 'every man climbs well.'

But now, bridged across the dièdre for all the world like a man straddling the hearth in his own home, he kept the rope tight and pursued this hypothetical retreat with methodical thoroughness.

Above the pendule the fault closed for nearly seventy metres. That would be the critical passage. All the roping down would be hazardous. But a rappel of that length over blank rock would demand inexorable accuracy. In a blizzard there would be no room for error. A slow agonising withdrawal; hours of waiting in the bitter weather; hunger, cold; they would have to endure all that. He knew how quickly determination dies in exhausted men. Civilised creatures (he knew it to his cost) were not good at surviving. And since experience had taught him never to expect too much from his companions, he thought it probable that he would have to provide the willpower for them all.

He considered all of this. He considered it, and he dismissed it. The sky was empty. The wind blew from the north-east. Beyond the shadow of the face the sun shone above the forest and in the meadow. There would be no disaster. But if it came he would know what to do.

But now his second had arrived at the stance. He paused just below the shoulder, took one hand from the crack, and passed his belay sling to the leader who clipped it into a karabiner. Then he surveyed the wastes of the great wall.

'Now it gets hard?' he asked.

'Yes,' said Raymond. 'Now it gets hard.'

All around them the wind stirred uneasily. Swaying the ropes and étriers. Ruffling their clothes. Daniel said nothing. But he sensed a rigour in this constant, restless movement. It disturbed him. He knew that they had reached a point of departure. Now, at last, the face fulfilled its reputation. Above them, in ever diminishing perspective, lay the dièdre. Like a stony track crossing a desert where nothing lived for long. The storms which swept the face killed everything. He turned his mind aside, thankful he was not required to lead what lay ahead, and worked silently, laying out the light rappel rope and securing the big sac which they would have to haul up the crucial pitches.

It was very cold. His fingers moved clumsily in the bitter air. It took him a long time to do what was necessary.

All this while Raymond crouched at the top of his étriers, cigarette in hand, waiting stolidly for everything to be prepared. But he was not unconcerned. For him the next few hours would be critical. To stand here – not there. To act now – instead of then. Such things would determine whether he lived or died. Indeed, they were of the very nature of his life. He had endured stonefall, storm and avalanche. He had witnessed the pain of those he'd helped to carry down from the glaciers. He knew the good things which gave him joy, and the evil things which he fought against when he could and endured when he couldn't. And he sensed, in the bodies of the dead, in the canvas shrouds he'd helped to drag to the valley, the taste of tyranny at the heart of things. His life was so entirely circumscribed, so touched at every point by its presence, that he had come to see all living things in terms of mortality. And he suffered a profound sense of wrongness.

He had taken possession of his death. Now it occupied him like a disease. So he lived outside it, externally, stretched around a dark interior void. How to recover himself– that was his perpetual torment. But that moment of grace seemed granted only when conditions threatened survival. And after such effort that, extended to the limit of endurance, he could sustain it only if he must succeed or perish.

Yet at such moments on the great faces he seemed to enter the holy place. There he might ask 'I?' And somewhere among the silent walls and pitted ice fields something seemed to answer '*Thou*!' Raymond was a sceptical man. He knew that confirmation was no more than an exalted extension of his own life. Yet it made no difference to his happiness. But he never spoke of that.

I cannot speak about that, he sometimes told himself: I cannot put that into words.

But he could feel it. He felt it now, through his hands shifting in the crack, in the pressure of granite varying against his knuckles, at sudden resistance to his toes twisted and pushed downwards. And more than anything did he feel it, now, with every movement of the wind. At this height it prowled constantly about the face. And he welcomed it, rejoiced at its noise all around him, enclosing his own harsh breathing, the scrape of his boots, the clinking of pegs and karabiners. He felt it pushing between his legs. It ruffled the sleeves of his cagoule, billowed the hood against the nape of his neck. Sometimes it struck so fiercely he was forced against the rock. Then he hung motionless, feeling the ropes plucking at his waist. Conscious of the mountain closed against him. When the wind dropped he climbed on.

The protrusion of the walls on either side of the crack was so slight as to be almost useless. Occasionally he saw tiny holds on the face, or chipped from the edge of the fault, but he chose not to use them. He climbed swiftly, with a rhythm that a practised man falls into unthinkingly, seeming to impose upon the crack's dimensions a regularity that wasn't really there. At every move his hands shaped to fit the configuration of the rock: sometimes clenched and twisted; sometimes open, with the fingers straight, or partly bent; sometimes with the thumb splayed across the index finger and the knuckles pressed hard against the granite. At every move he pulled against the jammed fist. Each time, he felt the coarse rock rasp across the backs of his hands. He felt it but it did not occur to him to think of it as painful. He could hang, if necessary, for five or six minutes from one jammed hand before the pain began to matter.

Daniel sat in étriers facing the rock. He heard the Czechs below him, their voices blown about by the wind which crashed now in waves against the face. With every shock he felt the doubled rope snatched violently, saw the man above him shrink against the rock. The wind poured over him. He could feel it streaming from his clothes.

'What about this wind?' he shouted.

'What?'

'This wind.'

'What about it?'

Daniel shook his head. The rope began to move again, and he guided it awkwardly through the karabiner with his gloved hand. He was cold. His neck ached from looking upwards. His knees were sore. Each thigh throbbed painfully. He peered down between his legs to where the Czechs were waiting thirty metres below, pressed against the wall. The red, woollen hat bobbed above an outflung arm as the giant pointed to something a long way off across the glacier. 'Hey! Tomas!' he shouted.

The giant looked up and waved, but whatever he shouted drowned in a great roar of wind. Daniel strained to look.

He had to lean back against the pull of the sling at his chest.

As he turned his head the wind struck his face so violently that he raised a shoulder to protect himself. He could see nothing. The sky was as vast and empty as the Russian steppes he'd read about in books. But then, behind the wind, he heard the sharp banging of a hammer. He felt the ropes pulled up urgently. He let them go until all the slack was taken up. Then he prepared the big sac for its ascent. It gave a lot of trouble. It flew across the face threatening to drag Raymond from the rungs of his étriers. Then he cursed, shouting angrily at Daniel, and leant far back on his belay, holding the sac's weight on one arm, gesticulating wildly with the other.

But when the sac had been hauled up to the stance, it was a great relief to Daniel. He was free of it for the first time that day. As he began the pitch he felt quite different. It wasn't as hard as he'd expected. The jams were very good. His boots wedged securely at each thrust of the foot. He looked across the face to the north-west and saw the great peaks of the Oberland, range upon range, receding in the blue haze. All the old delight flowed hack again.

When he was very young, lying in the long dormitory just before he went to sleep, he used to imagine the acrobats. He was supposed to think about the Four Last Things. He tried to do so; he was an obedient child. But Death, the Judgement, Heaven and Hell were totally eclipsed by those marvellous bodies. They were not ordinary performers. They had no identity. No sex, no colour. Not even faces. They swept from bar to bar like birds. They flicked their bodies upwards in impossible somersaults, turned, dropped, twisted, fell in tumbling circles, stopped at the turn of a wrist, motionless, poised upon a rail. They never failed. They mastered nothing. They seemed happy simply to be there.

Below him the Czechs were on the move again. He caught snatches of deep voices drifting up on the wind. Whenever he looked up he saw the rope as solid as a hawser and beyond it squatted his companion, durable as ever, like an old boulder wedged across the crack. Only his hands moved, taking in the rope. At his lips a cigarette flickered. Daniel rejoiced. About him were men who worked, called to one another, drove out loneliness; and though they could not banish fear, they made it bearable. The wind battered him relentlessly. And he cursed it, as climbers do. But it no longer troubled him. He huddled against the face whenever it struck him, and when it dropped, he climbed on.

All this time Raymond was thinking of the pitch immediately above. He knew all the famous pitches on the classic routes: the *Fissure de la Grand-Mère* on the Ryan Arête of the Aiguille de Plan, the *Lambert Crack* on the Dru, the *Lépiney* on the Peigne, the *Fissure Fix* and the *Fissure Brown* on the Blaitière. But no one had given a proper name to the sestogrado crack. Not even Schiavi. He'd spoken to him of it only the previous summer in Courmayeur. He spent a whole evening on the terrace of Schiavi's house in the Val di Ferret drinking *bocca nera* while the sun traversed the summits of the Grandes Jorasses. They sat together watching the last turrets washed with a light like cognac and the snowfields turning a ghostly blue beneath rich, black shadows which crept across the face.

The old Italian had a bald, curiously flattened skull. His skin was very brown and wrinkled. He looked out at the mountains of his valley from behind black, impenetrable glasses. Like an old lizard. Motionless, relaxing upon his terrace in the evening sun. He sat with one arm resting upon the table, his maimed hand crooked about the glass. He sipped his black, bitter drink and when he spoke it was in a low sibilant voice.

Yes! Up there was the Rifugio Gervasutti. Giusto's hut. Il grandissimo Giusto. Killed thirty years ago. Of Rinuccini and his brother he said nothing. But he spoke of Morra, his old companion. Old Morra! Still climbing as well as ever. And while he spoke Raymond was thinking of his first climb up there on the Grandes Jorasses by the Crete des Hirondelles many years ago. And of the swallows the Englishman wrote about so movingly. Dead swallows on the col. But there never were any swallows. It was all a joke. An English joke!

'The sestogrado crack? *Non, vieux!* I did not climb it. I survived it. Jamais encore. *C'est feroce, ça! C'est un passage d'une rigueur exceptionnelle.*'

The old guide shuddered. But whether it was the memory of the crack, or of poor Rinuccini, or simply a chill in the night air, Raymond never knew.

He watched impatiently as the small man struggled up the last few metres. Possessed now by a restless tension (*Nervenpfeffer*, the Munich men call it) he was anxious to begin. Yet he supervised the complicated changeover at the end of the pitch with customary caution. He checked the belays, ensured the solidity of the pegs (they were particularly secure) and seemed to Daniel to take an unconscionable time over the minutest details. But when, at last, he was satisfied he went swiftly.

For the first few metres there was no significant change. Except, perhaps, that the wall was flatter, more vertical. Then, gradually, the crack widened. He became aware that he was climbing an outer layer of rock which clung to the mountain's core like the split skin of an onion. The inner recess of the fissure was blocked, now, by some interior wall of a particularly coarse, crystalline granite. At each corner was a thin crack which might have taken a peg had it been possible to place one. He had pegs small enough. But he would have had to place them almost flat against the inner wall and it was quite impossible to strike them at such an angle. He worked with his left arm and leg wedged in the crack, gripping the sharp edge with his right hand high above his head, pulling strenuously to keep himself from toppling backwards. His right leg scuffled uselessly against the wall. The further he progressed the shallower the crack became. After fifteen metres' intense struggle there was room for no more than half a boot, and the width of a forearm. And he was still without protection. He felt the first flicker of alarm. He was not yet halfway up. He could not possibly climb such a pitch without a rest. In his forearm the great flexor muscle threatened to collapse at any moment. He needed desperately to relax. He looked down swiftly. His second seemed a very long way off. Raymond saw Daniel's face, bearded and dark under the red helmet, staring up at him intently, and he knew that if he couldn't place a peg within the next few metres he would have to go down.

He began the struggle again, knowing that every movement upward lessened his chances of a safe retreat. But at last he found a hairline fracture at the back of the crack. It took him several minutes to get the piton in. He had to hammer it left-handed, and since this placed an intolerable strain upon his right arm, which alone held him upright, he was forced to work in stages, wedging his left arm back in the crack every few seconds. But the piton would go no more than a couple of centimetres into the rock and it cost him such an effort that there could be no question, any longer, of a retreat. He clipped the foot-sling into the tiny peg, and held his breath as he stepped into it. It jerked fractionally downward. He froze. The peg's bright eye stared back at him.

'Gently,' he shouted. 'Gently, for Christ's sake!'

But it held. He felt the rope tighten at his waist, drawing him up to the rock. He stood in the sling, his right arm hanging limply, his left still wedged, head bowed, resting against the crack. He stayed like that for a long time.

When he began again he had advanced no further than two metres before he heard the sharp, metallic note of the piton flying out.

He stopped. For a moment he considered whether he should replace it. A fall from this point would be very serious. On the other hand to replace it would make fresh demands upon his strength. He wasn't sure he could afford that. In any case he doubted whether the peg would hold even a slight fall. There would certainly be an opportunity for another, for he was quite sure nobody, neither Schiavi, nor anybody else, could have climbed this pitch without direct aid. Nevertheless he ran out twenty-five metres of rope before he was able to place the next peg, a small 'ace of spades' which went in no further than the last, and by the time he'd hammered home the third, five metres from the top of the passage, he was almost exhausted.

From time to time Daniel would call to him encouragingly, 'How's it going?' Raymond did not reply.

He took a long rest at the third peg. The worst was still to come. He was well aware of that. But it was not until he raised his head to take stock of the situation that he realised how critical his position really was. Away to the right, perhaps eight metres and slightly lower down, was the flake, the sole link with the upper section of the central face. To reach it he would have to place a peg high in the crack, clip into it, and make a pendulum swing across the wall. This much he knew already. He knew, also, that to make the pendule successfully he would need to climb as high as possible above the level of the flake. But he was quite unprepared for the conditions in which the manoeuvre would have to be performed, for the crack closed abruptly just above his head. It simply ceased. It was as if a door had been slammed in his face. The rock above him was holdless and slightly overhanging. He could see the whole section, even Schiavi's pendule point, a rusted peg, well buried, perhaps five metres off. Between him and it there was nothing but a thin fracture a few centimetres long, scarred where a peg had formerly been placed. It was a full three metres away. The peg itself was missing.

It was then he realised, with horror, what the passage actually proposed. The next peg had to be placed by his second. He could see no alternative. He would have to bring up Daniel who might then climb over him to gain the necessary height.

The thought of it, of the whole manoeuvre resting on the security of one small 'ace of spades' (and that only half buried) appalled him. For a moment he considered the possibility of traversing directly to the flake. A glance at the wall dissuaded him. In any case he knew that Daniel could never climb the crack without direct aid from the rope. And to bring him up belayed from the flake, with the rope passing through the peg at a right angle, would throw all the load against its weakest point. The weight would force it sideways. It would fail.

Wearily he descended to the bottom rung of his étrier. He clipped another below it. Then he examined the peg. It seemed as frail as silver. But it was lodged sturdily in the horizontal crack and as long as the pull stayed vertical it would hold. He decided to put in another by its side. He did so, but he could force it in no further than the first. He clipped two karabiners to it. To one of these he tied back the white rope so that it hung vertically down the side of the crack. He unfastened the red rope from the first peg and passed it through the other karabiner. Then he belayed himself with a short sling. He arranged his étriers so that he could sit back with one leg in the first and his other leg bent behind him in the second. He turned his head and shoulders sideways and called down to Daniel.

'I shall have to bring you up,' he shouted.

He didn't say why.

'What about the sac?'

'Oh, Christ!'

There was no room for the sac. There was no room for another peg, either. He reached behind him, unclipped the light, 9 mm rappel rope from his back and re-fastened it at the front of his waist. Then he began another weary haul, fighting both the sac and the wind every centimetre of the way. When it arrived he simply clipped it to the last rung of the étrier on which he stood. Then he called to Daniel again.

'You'll have to stay there for a bit.'

Exhausted already, he thought, with the worst of it yet to come.

But it was a great relief to be doing nothing. He rested for a while, sitting idly in the étriers and thought of that old Italian drinking *bocca nera* on his terrace, black glasses turned to the Grandes Jorasses. When the wind dropped he lit a cigarette, and with the charred match he sketched a slogan on the smooth granite wall: SCHIAVI – LUNATIC.

All the way up he kept his second on a tight rope. Daniel slipped continually. Had to grab again and again at the fixed rope. He was forced twice to tie a loop to rest in. At times he stopped altogether, considered, changed position, floundered, failed, changed again, while Raymond waited wearily, eyes fixed upon the pegs, wondering just how much longer it would be before they both fell.

He was bitterly cold. The wind enclosed him like a shroud. It blurred the sharp edges of things. Ropes, gloves, fingers blurred together. He ceased to feel the rung cutting his thigh. He had a sense of life retreating from the surface. He felt as if he were suspended in the act of falling backwards.

Only the wind supported him, turning him to a stone fixed in the ice. But at intervals, like noises in a mist, he heard an erratic scuffling beneath him, the creak of ropes twisting under strain. They were courting disaster. He was sure of it. All his instincts urged him to move on. But the next move depended upon Daniel. So he held himself in check. He treated Daniel with great patience.

'OK,' he said. 'It doesn't matter. Take your time.'

But someone had to suffer for it, and since he would not permit himself to curse his second, he cursed Schiavi instead. He could not imagine how Schiavi had climbed this pitch. He wasn't big enough. He remembered now asking him about that – about the long reach at the top.

'How did you manage it?'

'I grew!' said the Italian, with a grin.

When Daniel arrived he was very subdued. He clipped his étriers to one of the karabiners that hung down beneath the white rope, climbed into them, and listened as Raymond told him, simply, what he wanted him to do. Daniel heard him in silence.

'I'll do my best,' he said.

He took the light hammer from his hip pocket and slung it from a short cord on his wrist. It was copied from a Stubai which he'd taken to the blacksmith at home.

'Can you make one like this,' he'd asked, 'but lighter?'

So the blacksmith made it and burnt his initials on the shaft. *Fabrique par JN.* They had both been very proud of it. Daniel had used it in the Alps for nearly twelve years. It was the only piece of equipment he had never renewed. Now he turned sideways in the étrier to take a peg.

'It'll be an extra-flat,' said Raymond.

Daniel found one of medium length, unclipped it. 'You'd better take a short one, too.'

He did so. He put it between his teeth. It was hard. Icy cold. He gripped it tightly and climbed to the top of the étrier. Then, bent double, his right hand grasping the karabiner, he stepped across on to Raymond's shoulder and began the delicate manoeuvre to stand upright. For the first time he was in front of the rope. He heard, through the wind, the harsh gasping of his companion as he strove to bear on his body the great weight. His position was extremely precarious. Raymond's body sagged at each thrust and the wind veered so erratically that he had to fit every movement to the changing currents. But he moved so delicately, was so absorbed in the austere discipline of the moment, that he felt no anxiety at all. Bit by bit Daniel levered himself upright. At last he stood astride Raymond's head, with his arms resting on the wall. The rock swayed from side to side beneath his hands. He took the piton from his mouth.

'Hold on!' he said. 'Not long now.'

He reached for the thin crack. But Raymond's body dipped suddenly. Daniel was thrown off balance and had to grab for the wall. He rested there, head turned sideways, pressing against the rock. He could see the pegs under his feet and the taut ropes and, a long way down, the red flash of the giant's hat. Then he put the piton between his teeth and began again, this time sliding both arms up the wall until the fingers of his left hand locked in the crack.

It was a long time before the piton was finally placed. But it needed a great exertion of will to strike the peg gently. Not to hurry. To hold back from a full swing. All this while Raymond was thinking, not for the first time, that he was getting too old for this sort of thing. A shoulder on a safe stance was one thing. But in étriers, on one half buried 'ace of spades', it was an extravagance that became less excusable as one got older. Yet it never occurred to him to complain. His second would do what had to be done as quickly as he could. His left leg was hurting acutely. It felt as if the blood hadn't flowed there for some time. But with Daniel trampling about on top of him, his whole body was so thrust down against the flexed limb that there was no possibility of relief. So the pain continued, sharpening all the time. Daniel seemed to have been banging for ages. You'll have to come down for a bit, he was about to say, when the banging stopped.

'How far … ' he began.

'All the way,' shouted Daniel triumphantly. 'Shall I go on?'

'No! No! Come down.'

'As you wish.'

Daniel clipped an étrier to the new peg before he left it and then started to reverse the manoeuvre. As he did so Raymond looked at the comfortable flake away to his right and made up his mind to eat something, and rest when he got there. He really wanted to think about that now. But he kept the ropes tight instead and began unravelling the complexities of the pendule that lay ahead.

Traditionally, a pendule of this kind precluded retreat. After such a move, say, on the west face of the Grepon, or the south ridge of the Aiguille Noire de Peuterey, one was committed. The strategy, according to Schiavi, was self-evident: one left a rope in position. Either at the pendule, for a swing back across the wall, or at the top of the crack, for a hand traverse back from the flake. But it was not self-evident to the leader. He placed no confidence in fixed ropes. Anything could happen. One invariably wanted them when the weather was at its worst. He had no intention of leading a retreat through stone fall, storm and lightning to the security of a fixed rope that wasn't there. One might as well jump off.

'Where will you fix it?' asked Daniel.

'What?'

'The rope.'

'I shan't.'

He stood up in the étrier, but when he tried to move his left leg it hurt so much he could barely straighten it.

'If we have to, we rope straight down the wall.'

He unfastened the buckle below his knee and began to rub the leg vigorously.

But it was more than seventy metres down the wall. There were no stances anywhere. They would need to make three rappels to reach the ledge above the chimney. Each one from pegs.

Daniel looked at him doubtfully.

'Seventy metres?' he asked.

'Seventy metres!'

His leg felt a little easier. He pushed the red sock down to his ankle and let the buckle and strap hang loose about his calf. Then he began, stiffly, the climb up to the pendule point.

Unhappily Daniel watched him go. He would have preferred a fixed rope. He could not understand why Raymond had dismissed it. He was wrong. Despite his profound respect for Raymond he thought him wrong. And to be wrong here, in such a place …

Then he remembered the guardian at the Cabane des Planches. An old man not right in the head, perhaps. But what he said was true. Nothing guarantees survival. ('It'll catch up with him one day,' he said, 'you'll see!') And when you thought about it you could see how it would happen. How could *he* marry – or keep a shop? Or serve tourists in a small hotel? The security of the valley, that ultimate comfort of the older guides – it meant nothing to him. He would go on until the end came. Like Lionel. A matter of luck. A jammed rope that suddenly gives way, a rappel sling that's rotten, the hidden crevasse. Gervasutti … Lehmann … Lachenal … The best men did these things. It would begin on a day like any other day. High winds, perhaps, and bitter cold, like any other day. Hours of exposure on difficult rock, struggling to stay upright, striving to read the signs properly, to make the right choice. Exhaustion at noon, or nightfall. The last split second of collapse …

'At … ten … tion!'

He looked up.

'*Vorsicht!*' he shouted. '*Seil!*'

Past him flashed the eighty-metre rappel rope. It fell clear of Jaro, bounced in mid-air, and dropped its last coils a metre short of the giant's hat.

If the Czechs were startled they didn't show it. The giant made no move at all. Halfway up the crack, poised above the first peg, the Oberland cap opened suddenly like a lid for a dark face to peer upward, then dropped again as Jaro resumed the pitch. He climbed it like Raymond but with less apparent effort. He kept his body straight and despite the great strain on his right arm he never faltered. He looked very good.

They'll fix a rope to the flake, Daniel told himself. They're bound to.

As he made his preparations for the pendule Raymond felt a great emptiness. The crack had nearly finished him. A desperate man on critical rock, clutching and hoping. He had been reduced to that.

Among the best in Europe, he told himself. *The Route Major*, the Walker Spur, the North Face of the Matterhorn, the Red Pillar of Brouillard, the Pear

Buttress, the Peigne, the Verte, the Dru; a host of others. Names that were like decorations. Remembered without vanity, out of simple pride, so that he might recover what was lost.

Now they seemed like old battles that no longer mattered. (It was in the nature of old battles, he recognised, not to matter – except to old men.) Even the Plan, where his brother died (where everyone died except Varaud and himself), that disaster that had nothing to do with luck or anything less than sheer determination to survive. Even that was not enough. He had nothing left to hold back the weariness, to halt the conviction of strength fading, of the mind letting go. One day it would probably begin like this. He saw now how it might happen. A man might arrive exhausted at the top of the crack and fail at the pendule, keep missing it until he stopped trying.

Yet the crack, at least, was finished. It lay behind him. And he knew exactly what had to be done now. He must cross the wall at the first attempt. He could take a long rest at the flake. He could eat something. At the flake he could restore himself. One swing across the wall would put him right.

He threaded the doubled rappel rope through the descendeur (it was English, shaped in a figure-of-eight, the gift of an English climber who admired him). He clipped it to his waist and looked down. Daniel was back on the étriers five metres below. He was watching the Czechs. The flake seemed a very long way off. To gain enough momentum he would have to descend diagonally, away from it. On the wall below him, to the left, was a yellow patch shaped like a huge fist. Slowly he lowered himself, inching the rope through the descendeur, his feet pushing him far over to the left. Daniel was looking up now but the leader saw neither him nor the Czechs. He saw only the flake, and the grey rock passing beneath his boots. The further he descended the more difficult it became. The wind beat at him constantly. At last he could no longer hold himself. He let go. Then, when the rope swung, leaped, and as his body dropped, ran down across the wall. Almost immediately he saw that he was going to miss it. As the run carried him beneath its lower edge he grabbed with his right hand for a projection, swung for a moment, hauled himself up on to the flake and sank down beside it. There he crouched, wedged in the narrow gap between the flake and the great wall, his body shaken by a violent spasm of weeping.

It was dark behind the flake. Still. All sounds muffled. Like a door closed against the wind. When he recovered, after a few seconds, he seemed to hear a ragged noise of cheering. He scrambled up a little in the flake and half turned to look down. They were all cheering. Daniel had released the climbing ropes and hung back on his sling, waving both arms. Jaro, who had no arms to wave with, gazed benevolently from his lodging in the crack, and many metres below the giant waved his red hat, while a far-off excited voice shouted 'Allez la France! Allez la France!' over and over again.

They spent a long time at the flake. Daniel crossed easily on one fixed line of the rappel rope. Jaro followed him, singing exultantly. He left a short, ten-metre rope behind him just as Daniel had expected. When the giant crossed, all four of them were wedged together in the narrow gap like peas in a pod. The wind no longer troubled them. In this safe shelter the perils of the north wall (for a time, at least) might be forgotten.

Daniel scrambled deep into the recess and found a ledge for the stove to rest on. They passed mugs of coffee from hand to hand. They ate chocolate and biscuits. Jaro offered them the English cigarettes he'd bought at the Swiss border. Each man told of his fears at the pendule, crack or slab – and though they scarcely understood one another they laughed none the less. Raymond laughed with them. Jaro struck up his triumphant song again. He sang in German, in a fine deep voice, singing (so it seemed to Daniel) of joy and brotherhood and friendship, in that emphatic tongue. And Tomas joined in, too. Raymond sang with them. And the sound of their singing swelled in the narrow space behind the flake until the rock rang and the sound, redoubled, echoed across the face.

Daniel longed to join them. But he couldn't. He didn't know the words. In his excitement he longed to do something. He took a sharp flint from the debris behind the flake and scratched their names, and the initials of their countries, on the wall. None of them could remember the date so Daniel consulted his pocket diary (he took it with him everywhere). It was the fifteenth. The feast of the Assumption. He scraped it in white scratches on the dark rock. He produced a photograph from inside the diary and showed it to Tomas.

'*Mein Kind*,' he said. 'It's his birthday soon. *Sein Geburtstag*.'

'*Wie alt?*' asked Jaro.

'*Sechs!*' said Daniel. 'He'll be six.'

He explained that he'd be home for that. He wouldn't miss that. He spoke of the child with great joy. As he did so Raymond remembered that just two days would bring another anniversary. The seventeenth of August. The date which used to be dreaded by the old guides of Mont Blanc. *Le jour malheureux* – on which they would never climb. It was also the anniversary of his brother's death.

6 Chapter 6

All through the long afternoon the ascent continued. They climbed the edge of the flake, crossed the return traverse and began once more up the dièdre. Hour after hour, pitch after pitch, on rock of the fifth grade they climbed for well over 200 metres, with every stance in étriers, every belay hammered in the crack. They were still two separate ropes. Sometimes seventy or eighty metres separated the first man from the fourth. They were scarcely ever close enough to touch. But they climbed together now. Their voices echoed up and down the great wall as they called to one another. While the mountain slept, Daniel thought, like some gigantic beast – they were marching into its lair.

At last, in the evening, Raymond halted beneath the ten-metre roof. The wind had dropped a little but still came in from the north-west. There were no clouds. The sun was slipping down. To the north and west a hazy blue obscured the horizon.

It was cold and dark under the roof. He had expected to find ice, and he was not mistaken. The split rock looked as if it had been stuck together with a smooth cement. Pitons fixed in an ice-filled crack will not hold for long. So he attacked the ice with the north wall hammer, hitting upwards, chipping the long pick patiently into the crack (knocking his helmet several times against the roof). Tiny particles of the fractured ice stung his face and pattered on top of the helmet.

The larger lumps dropped past him straight to the glacier, 800 metres below. He crossed the roof an arm's length at a time, clearing the ice, driving pitons up into the crack, fixing the new tapes he'd brought specially for the roof (the new nylon webbing tapes with loops for the feet: once fixed they could be left in place).

As he swung from one tape to the next his helmet hit the roof again, hard this time, and was forced down sideways on to his cheek. He felt the buckle go. Now it kept slipping as he swayed about under the roof. He kept pushing it back, fuming, sweating with exertion. It was cold under the roof and the sweat felt cold and clammy on his back and shoulders. He was alarmed that he might lose it altogether. Eventually he had to take it off and fasten it to his waist-loop.

But all this took a long time. And all the while the sun was dipping round and down.

Under the massive canopy of the roof Daniel (and Tomas, a few metres below) was cut off from the sight and sound of anything above. They could have heard nothing beyond the crash of Raymond's north wall hammer and the splintering of ice. But Jaro, a long way down the face, caught the first faint rumble. Like gunfire. At first he couldn't tell whether it was ice or stone that flashed past him, well out from the wall. Seconds later he was struck on the arm. He called out to warn them.

'*Vorsicht!*' he shouted. '*Steinschlag!*'

They looked down at him and waved.

But Raymond knew what would be happening above him. He felt the first flicker of alarm. It was the familiar warning. And the fact that he should feel it now made him more uneasy. He should have crossed the overhang at least an hour earlier. He even considered stopping under the roof till morning. But the thought of a bitter night in étriers, instead of the sheltered cave beyond the glacis, only a few metres away, persuaded him. It wasn't far. Just a few more minutes.

Then he could see to the helmet. So he worked on. At eight o'clock he passed uneasily beyond the lip of the roof.

Daniel felt the ropes taken up and tightened. He heard the leader's voice calling him to come on. He, too, thought of the cave, a meal, and a night's rest only a few minutes away.

As he unclipped his first étrier from the wall he heard a dry, distant clattering – then a drawn-out shout drowning in a rolling, thunderous roar. Oh, Christ! (he knew what it was) and then the most appalling explosion shook the roof and he clung in terror to his one remaining étrier, his face buried in his arms as lorry-loads of rubble poured from the rock …

Oh my God, he began … *oh, my God* … mumbling the act of contrition, getting no further than the first few words as tons of rubble poured from the rock. Sun, air, everything was blotted out. Thick, choking dust filled everything. He could see nothing. As the dreadful noise receded down the face he heard, emerging from it, a voice shouting the same thing over and over again. Then he realised he was still alive (was he hurt? he didn't feel hurt) and that Jaro, at least, was still alive because that was his voice shouting.

'*Der Führer ist gefallen! Der Führer ist gefallen!*' Over and over again. That's what it sounded like.

He was still too stunned to realise what had happened. Then there was another voice, closer this time, shouting in the strange language. He saw a murky shape flattened against the wall a few metres below. It was Tomas shouting at him. Calling out in German and saying, 'Get up to him! For God's sake get up to him!' Then, as the light came back, he saw two lines of climbing rope sliding gently down towards him over the lip of the roof.

He had a hand and foot in the first tape when he realised that Tomas was still shouting at him.

'*Ihr Seil! Geben Sie mir Ihr Seil!*'

But Daniel daren't untie the rope. Raymond might slide over the edge at any moment.

'What rope?' he shouted.

He didn't understand.

'I can't untie the rope.'

'*Ihr Seil! Geben Sie es mir!*'

The rappel rope! That was what he meant. He stepped back on to the étrier and clipped his sling to the peg. He took the coiled rope from the top of the sac, unfastened it, clipped one end to his waist loop and lowered the other end to Tomas. He didn't wait for the giant to tie on but set off immediately across the roof. He moved in panic, snatching at the nylon tapes, struggling to get his feet into the loops that swung aside as he lunged at them. Tomas watched him with alarm. After a couple of metres he gave a loud cry, twisted round in the tapes, and blundered back towards the wall. He stepped on to the étrier and opened the sac that hung beside it. It was packed full. For almost a minute he groped inside the sac. He was on the verge of tears. At last he found the little first aid box, stowed it in his anorak and started back across the roof.

Now he moved more steadily. Whenever he glanced down he saw the giant looking up at him, and the tiny figure of Jaro, waiting patiently a long way down the wall. He asked himself if he had done everything. He was roped to Tomas. He had the first aid box. He could leave the sac to the Czechs. He pulled the doubled climbing rope back through the karabiners until it hung down in two great loops beside him. If the leader slid over the edge at least he would not fall on to a slack rope. And there were half a dozen pegs to hold him. The nearer he got to the lip of the overhang the more difficult it became to move freely. Each time he stretched for the next tape the weight of the three ropes held him back. At last he reached the tapes at the edge of the roof.

He hesitated. Then, fearfully, he stuck his head out from under the rock. He saw a short, steep wall, the ropes trailing down. He could hear nothing.

He shouted.

His voice echoed from the face. He shouted again.

Nothing.

So, filled with dread, he stepped up on to the short wall. *Oh, Christ*! he thought. Don't let him be too badly hurt. Just below the top he paused again.

But nothing struck him. There was a smell of scorching. Fresh white scars pitted the glacis. Everything was still. The upper face dark and sombre. Like a gigantic monument against the sky. He saw the great walls of the dièdre towering. And Raymond's body, flung down before them.

He lay well back from the edge. So far back, Daniel thought, he should never have been struck. One arm flung out. The fair hair soaked with blood. A pool of blood still spreading under the head. It looked black in the failing light.

Must have been an odd stone, thought Daniel helplessly. When he reached Raymond, he had no idea what to do.

There was a dressing pad in the first aid tin. He remembered that. He took it out (Raymond, he saw, was breathing: was alive). Then, not knowing where to put it, he pressed the dressing where the blood seemed thickest and bandaged it (tightly? loosely? he didn't know) in place. Before he'd finished the black blood was welling up again. He covered Raymond with his anorak. There was nothing else he could do.

Tomas found him some minutes later, still crouched beside the body.

'I wanted to move him,' Daniel muttered.

He looked up at the giant.

'I thought his spine … '

Tomas said nothing. He took off his duvet and began to slide it under Raymond. Daniel moved to help but the giant shook his head.

'Jaro,' he said. And pointed to the glacis.

Obediently Daniel went down the glacis and drove in a peg.

First he had to haul the sacs. They were very heavy. He heard the sound of a heavy object dragging over the ledge, but he didn't look. He kept pulling in the sacs. When at last he turned around he saw that Raymond's body had gone. Only the pool of blood remained. He could still see it, even in the dark. He felt sick – was frightened he was going to be sick. He kept his eyes fixed on Jaro's rope moving spasmodically over the edge until at last the Czech came up.

'*Wie geht's?*' he asked.

Daniel shook his head.

They walked together to the cave at the foot of the dièdre. Dully Daniel saw that Raymond's gear – his hammer, his pegs and karabiners, his helmet – had been piled up at the entrance. A faint light gleamed on the helmet. It was dark in the cave. Tomas was working with the aid of a small torch. He had rebandaged Raymond's head, and now the bleeding seemed to have stopped. Raymond lay on the duvet with the torch on his chest, its beam directed at his arm. In the faint reflection from the walls of the cave his face was livid. Patches of black blood clotted his hair and beard. His eyes were closed. He looked at the point of death. Now Daniel saw for the first time that the arm was shattered, too. The sleeves of the anorak and the woollen shirt had been cut away at the shoulder. Tomas had dressed the arm and splinted it with half the demountable axe and three of the Charlet ice pitons. He was binding it to a small sling around Raymond's neck. Daniel looked at the little pile of bloodsoaked cloth and shut his eyes.

'*Er muss ins Krankenhaus.*'

It was all Tomas could say. And it was right – stupid though it seemed to him to say it in such a place. This poor man needed attention in a hospital. Tomas wanted to explain that the bones of the forearm were broken and displaced.

That they probably needed surgery. That the leader was suffering from shock. From concussion. Probably cerebral contusion. Possibly even more cerebral and cervical damage.

'*Er hat sich den Arm gebrochen,*' he said eventually.

He struggled vainly for more words. Then, in desperation, struck his head with his clenched fist.

Bewildered, Daniel turned to Jaro. The Czechs spoke together rapidly for several minutes. Then Jaro told him.

'*Ein Schädelbruch,*' he said.

A fractured skull! For a few moments there was silence. Tomas put his hand on the small man's shoulder.

'*Er ist ein sehr starker Mann,*' he said.

'How strong does he have to be?' asked Daniel bitterly. Tomas fell silent. Then he reached out and took the helmet. 'I can mend that,' said Daniel.

Tomas looked blank.

'Mend it,' Daniel repeated. He didn't know the German. He took the helmet and made the motion of sewing back the broken buckle.

Tomas smiled and nodded.

So he went out on the glacis. The moon was up. A few stars glittered in the frozen air. The ledge was like a landscape after a disaster. Sombre. Desolate. Littered with debris from the upper face. Nothing stirred.

He took his torch from the side pocket of the big sac and began to search for the flat tin which held the needles and the twine. Threading the needle was difficult with only the torch for light, but he got the twine through at last and began sewing back the buckle, running the needle through the holes in the leather strap. He had to peer at it closely in the torchlight. From time to time he looked back towards the tiny light moving eerily in the cave. If he stopped sewing he could hear the faint hiss of the stove, and voices talking quietly in a foreign tongue. For a moment he felt reassured. For a moment he closed his eyes and tried to pray, searching for the gentle images that made prayer feasible. But it was useless. Nothing came to him. Only the dull conviction that nothing – nothing at all – could change what had happened. It was all useless.

He heard the sound of a hammer. Jaro was breaking ice to melt on the stove.

Ice, and the thought of winter, evoked a memory of years ago. Fir trees. Oh, to grow … to grow … to get big and old … It was the tale of the little fir tree. To get big and old. He'd thought so too. To go into the marvellous great world. He remembered it all clearly: the thick, soft pages, illustrations which he coloured with his crayons … and the dreadful end. Thrown out. Trampled beneath the children's boots. Cast into the fire. He'd cried at that. And he remembered how he'd torn out the last few pages to make the story stop on Christmas Eve. But that was useless too. He knew how it really ended. That it finished in the shocking fact of death. Death and dismembering. Nothing could alter that.

But the buckle was finished. Tight again. He put his things back in the sac and took the helmet back to the cave. Raymond hadn't changed. He was still unconscious. The same harsh, rasping breathing. Carefully Tomas fastened the helmet on the bandaged head.

The ice melted quickly. But it shrank so much there was hardly enough water to fill two mugs. Wearily Daniel began to get up, but Jaro waved him back and went out again with the hammer and the torch.

No one had anything to say. Daniel listened to the chip – chip – chip of the hammer, and lit one cigarette after another (he offered one to Tomas but the giant shook his head). A thin steam rose from the water in the pan. Daniel crouched beside it, eyes closed, his mind fixed dully on the steady hiss of the stove as if it were the only comfortable thing he had. He scarcely heard Jaro come back into the cave. The noise of the stove enveloped him. His head drooped. The acrobats were coming back. Cautious. Shadowy. Like wild animals at dusk. He woke with a start. The leader was stirring. Not much. No more than a slight movement. A faint, protesting noise. A groan. By nine o'clock he had recovered consciousness.

He was very confused. When Tomas spoke to him in German he didn't seem to understand. Daniel tried. He translated the questions. Put them again and again, but with no result. Raymond wouldn't answer. He seemed to have no idea of what had happened. Sometimes he muttered to himself. The Aiguille du Plan seemed to be on his mind again. He groaned a good deal.

The questioning continued.

'Does it hurt here?'

'Does this hurt?'

'Can you move your toes?'

'Try to move your fingers.'

Jaro made a hot drink of concentrated milk and glucose. Raymond took it.

'What's the point of all this?' Daniel burst out despairingly. It's useless! Useless!'

But Tomas would not give up. He probed and manipulated, and laboured in broken German. So it went on. Step after step, by torchlight, in the frozen cave. When he was satisfied Tomas gave orders for the tent sac to be pegged to the wall of the cave. When this was done, and Raymond safely wrapped in his duvet and *pied d'elephant* inside the tent, Tomas told them what had happened. A probable fracture of the skull; no injury to the spine; the possibility of damage to the brain. He couldn't tell for certain. He would have to wait.

Raymond lay quietly in the tent. He didn't move much. Only the occasional noise. Now and then his head turned from side to side. His face was ashy pale. He was evidently in considerable pain.

Tomas sat with him in the tent while Jaro and Daniel settled to endure the cold as best they could. The Czechs had very little bivouac equipment. Jaro produced two large polythene bags. He offered one but Daniel refused it. He fastened up the hood of his duvet and crouched down in the *pied d'elephant*. Jaro squatted on his sac and gazed stolidly at the night. There was no wind. Nothing stirred. In the cave the air was solid. It bore down on everything. Breath vaporised and froze on the beard. The cold thrust between them. It severed all communication. After midnight there was silence. Each man withdrew into himself. As if life was only possible somewhere below the surface. In the darkness a match flared. A cigarette gleamed briefly beneath the hood, over lips fringed with ice. Daniel was facing the disaster. Bitterly he remembered the helmet. The ashen face fringed with blood. What a stupid thing to happen, he thought. Christ! What a bloody, silly stupid thing to happen.

7 Chapter 7

Jaro was the first to stir. He woke to the rank smell of sweat, to the stale remains of a weary day, and a night spent cramped in the plastic bag. His muscles ached. His hands shifting under the cagoule were damp and grimy. For some moments more he contrived to slip back from the grip of the new day. But his hands hurt. His bladder pressed him unremittingly. He struggled upright, stretching his stiff limbs, scratching his scalp with ragged fingernails. He lit the last of his English cigarettes. Then he went out on to the glacis.

It was the strangest dawn he had ever seen. Everything was flooded with green. It looked as if the earth was under water. Everything washed with the same green glow. Isolated clumps of fog clung to the land-like pockets of green gas. As he watched, a flight of birds wheeled from the upper meadows, dropped over the great cliff of the moraine and settled down the valley.

Jaro shivered violently. He stood against the rock to urinate, and glanced around. He noted the condition of the face and the peculiar tint of green now diminishing in the eastern sky. His water froze over the rock in a thin, black glaze. Nothing had changed. He was reassured. He went back to the cave. Then he remembered the accident.

He paused, turned to the tent, hesitated, then knelt at the entrance. He listened intently. He could hear nothing.

Daniel was still asleep, too. He lay huddled against the back wall, his knees drawn up to his chest. Jaro didn't wake him. He went to light the stove.

There was still some water frozen in the pan but the stove was empty. He opened his sac and shoved his hand down to the bottom. His fingers pushed through layers of clothing, encountered the shaft of an ice piton – then, impaled on its point, the small polythene bottle of cooking fuel. A sticky, glutinous mess covered the bottom of the sac. Miserably he removed the clothes and shook out the rest of the contents on to the floor of the glacis outside the cave. Bread, butter, cheese, sausage, even blocks of concentrated food: everything was saturated with the fuel. A tin of coffee, a small cylinder of glucose tablets and a tube of milk were all that remained. And he couldn't even light the stove.

He stood holding the empty sac in one hand, staring down at the little heap of spoilt food.

When Daniel woke it was to hear the Czechs talking quietly. He sat up.

'How is he?' he asked.

Tomas turned his head. He looked very low.

'*Er schläft*,' he said quietly.

Daniel dragged the stiffened bivouac sac from his legs. Across his back and breast, and down the length of his arms, his long-cramped muscles ached at the effort. The folds of the cagoule he wore over his duvet were seamed with frost that crackled as he went shivering to the bivouac tent. Gently, with a minimum of noise, he pulled the entrance open and pushed his head inside. But Raymond was not asleep. He was sitting up, his back propped on the climbing sac. He sat quite still. His eyes were open. His face, under four days' growth of beard, was grey and dirty, and gleamed with sweat. The eyes and mouth reflected nothing. It frightened Daniel.

'How is it?' he whispered. 'Is there anything to eat?'

His voice was just the same. Daniel was surprised.

'Right!' he said.

He withdrew from the tent. He felt relieved. The Czechs had turned away from the little pile of ruined food. On the glacis Jaro was laying out the pegs and wedges he would need in the hundred-metre corner. At the mouth of the cave stood Tomas, watching him. It was a bright, cold morning. Seeing them both together like that, tired, dejected, in ill-fitting clothes (all the more vulnerable for the frail vanities of a red woollen hat, and a fine white cap from the Oberland) Daniel felt suddenly the great weight of the wall above them. It was far from over.

Then he saw the food, and the polythene container still pinned on the ice piton, and the cold stove.

'You're not eating?' he said to Tomas.

The giant shrugged and jerked his thumb at the ground.

'*Sie müssen essen!*' said Daniel.

He knelt down beside the big sac and fumbled with the cord.

'We have plenty,' he said.

It wasn't true. They had very little food.

He took a wrapped packet from the sac and held it out to Tomas who was about to take it when Jaro's voice cut fiercely between them.

'*Wir können nicht ihr Essen nehmen!*'

Daniel felt the harsh, emphatic collocation of ks and ns. Tomas hesitated, uncertainly.

'*Bitte!*' said Daniel mildly.

He tossed the packet back to Tomas who caught it automatically and then, to forestall all argument, he set their pan of frozen water on his own propane stove and (though he'd matches of his own) he asked Jaro to light the gas. Jaro got down on one knee beside the stove and felt for his pocket.

'*Hier!*' said the giant.

He held out his new Feudor. Jaro took it. He turned on the tap, flicked the little wheel of the Feudor and held out the small flame to the burner. The gas ignited with a tiny plop, sputtered uncertainly for a moment, then settled to a steady roar.

'*Danke!*' said Daniel.

For a while the three of them watched the ice subsiding in the pan, and the vapour rising from it, crouched there around the stove, not speaking, as if the roar of gas, the little flame and the sight of ice melting were cheerful things for them to hear and look at.

'We'll need some more,' said Daniel.

He spoke in his own tongue but Jaro understood him.

'*Eis!*' he said.

He half rose.

'*Ich werde es holen,*' said Tomas.

He took Daniel's hammer and went out on to the glacis.

When the meal was cooked and the coffee brewed Daniel took a pan and a mug into the tent.

'How are things?' Raymond asked.

'Fine. Can you manage this?'

'I hope so.'

'All right?'

'Fine!'

Daniel went back to his own meal.

When they had finished they all went back to the tent. Tomas went in. Jaro stayed at the entrance, ready to translate. Daniel squatted at his side. He heard the rustle of clothing and the brief exchanges of the two men. The giant's voice stumbling in German, Raymond's terse replies. And long intervals of silence. He noticed that the wind had dropped almost to a whisper. He could see right down the glacier, right over the great cliff of the moraine and down the valley to Molino (smoke rising above the village, wood fires burning, children waking to the bright cold day: except that there it would not be cold at all, not really cold, just a sharpness that disappears as the sun climbs over the mountains). He shivered.

'*Sehr kalt!*' said Jaro.

Daniel nodded. If he stepped off the glacis, he mused, he would fall over 800 metres to the glacier: then to be able, like the acrobats, to stand up and walk away … But it was all so far away. Again he felt the seriousness of his position. It was like waking to remember that nothing has changed. That yesterday's anxieties are not resolved by dreams. Nothing resolves itself.

At that moment Tomas crawled out of the tent. Now, with Jaro's help, he told Daniel what he must do. Several times in the night Raymond had passed out. He was sure the skull was fractured. The chance of further damage to the brain remained a possibility. They must remain here, on the glacis. The Czechs would go for the top. They were fit. It was a fine day. They would climb fast. By mid-afternoon they would reach the summit. They would get help, medical aid, equipment. Tomorrow, at first light, they would be back. All would be well. He was emphatic about that.

'*Alles wird in Ordnung sein!*' said Jaro firmly. '*Alles wird in Ordnung sein!*'

Had Raymond heard all this he would have smiled. He was not capable of such simple faith. They were still 500 metres from the top. Much of the climbing was of the fifth grade, and the hundred-metre corner still lay ahead. But Daniel listened gravely to Tomas' assurances that all would be well. He helped them make the last few preparations, and when all was ready he lifted the big sac on to the giant's back. Jaro was the first to go.

'*Viel Glück, Herr Führer!*' he shouted towards the tent. Then he turned to Daniel and held out his hand. He didn't say anything but took off his cap and, in an odd gesture of embarrassment, drew his wrist across his forehead as if he were mopping his brow. Daniel shook his hand.

Jaro climbed easily up the inner, overhanging wall of the cave, jammed a hand into the crack that split its apex, pulled on it tentatively, then, when it held, jammed the other hand in the crack and swung out from under the roof. There, for a moment, he paused, hands buried in the rock, feet bridged across the mouth of the cave, his fine white cap slanting down from the wall.

'*Viel Glück!*' he shouted again.

Then he pulled powerfully up and on to the face. He worked swiftly, with brisk, precise movements of hands and feet in the crack, his pegs and wedges jangling under his arm as he climbed steadily higher.

The sun's up there, thought Daniel. He's heading for the sun.

He watched as Jaro ran out a full length of rope in so short a time, and all performed so easily, done with such delight, that he felt again the old, hopeless envy of all men who seemed freer, happier, more accomplished than himself. He remembered the pigeons on the road from Metz. Scores of pigeons fluttering from baskets by the roadside. How they'd wheeled in a great curving circle above the poplars and swung off south over the low hills of Alsace.

'Where are they going?'

'They're going home,' he'd said.

'Are they going to the mountains?'

The little boy could imagine no journey beyond the great valley of the Rhine which had any other purpose.

'They're going wherever their home is.'

'They're going to the mountains,' the child decided.

'We saw some pigeons, maman,' he'd cried. 'Going home to the mountains.'

She'd looked at *him* then, and he remembered wearily how futile it had seemed to explain that he'd said nothing … meant nothing at all. I'll write that down, he told himself impulsively. It must be possible to explain these things. When I get back, he thought, it will be different.

When the giant's turn came, and the ropes were taken up, he turned to face the cave and put both hands into the crack above his head. He was so big he could reach it without stepping off the glacis. He pulled on the jams experimentally, then turned back to shake hands.

'*Auf Wiedersehen!*'

'*Viel Glück!*' said Daniel.

'You have been very good to us,' he added in his own language. He wanted to say it in German, but he couldn't think of the words. The giant seemed to understand.

'*Wir müssen einander helfen,*' he said.

He clapped Daniel on the shoulder and turned to the rock.

'Tomas!' said Daniel suddenly. 'Don't forget us.'

The giant nodded. He would soon be back. All would be well.

'*Alles wird in Ordnung sein,*' he said again.

As he turned to the rock a deep voice rang out above their heads.

'*Allez la France!*' it shouted.

Daniel looked up and waved.

'*Viel Glück!*' he shouted.

Then, as Tomas began the long climb up to the stance, he went to the tent. He pushed his head through the sleeve entrance. Raymond had passed out again. He looked very pale. Daniel left him and went back to the glacis to watch the Czechs.

The giant was now no more than a small blue figure crawling purposefully up the vast expanse of the wall, while Jaro had shrunk so far back into a deeper part of the crack that an occasional flash of red against the grey rock was all that could be seen of him. Above them, seemingly immediately above but still a good way off, were the huge hanging buttresses which formed the walls of the great chimneys that gave entrance to the upper face.

'God!' said Daniel. 'It goes on for ever.'

He stood there for almost an hour until his neck ached from looking upward, staring after them as they receded between the buttresses which seemed blacker than ever to eyes screwed up against the light. He could hear Jaro's voice singing the great anthem he'd sung the day before. The words were indistinct and distorted, between the narrow walls. But the tune was there. Clear. Unmistakable. It stayed in his mind long after the voice that sang had faded from the central face. He remembered what Tomas had said jokingly of Jaro, as they drank coffee on the first morning.

'*Er wird der Böhmer Troll gennant!*'

It heartened him now to think of the Bohemian dwarf advancing resolutely through those dark chimneys. Bellowing his defiant hymn. Shattering whatever ice remained with shrewd blows of his hammer. They would come back soon. He was sure of it.

He turned away from the face. There would be a long time to wait before the Czechs returned. What a tale it will make then, he thought. A tale to scandalise the ancients at the Cafe des Nations, who placed such a trust in the inevitability of misfortune. And, though he would not have admitted it to anyone, it was a relief to think that for Raymond and himself the climb was over. Yet, alone on the glacis, he felt a little flat now that the Czechs were gone.

He settled to pass the time as best he could. There was much that he could find to do. He unpacked the two sacs and laid out the contents in neat, separate piles on the rock before the mouth of the cave. He refolded the clothing and replaced it in the big sac. He counted all the pegs and wedges and clipped them on to the karabiners according to their different types and sizes. He recoiled the ropes. He collected fresh ice from the glacis. He checked the food. Coffee, sugar, some tubes of milk, some cheese, a few biscuits and raisins, an end of sausage, and two bars of concentrated rations. It wasn't much. But it would be enough. The gas canister on the propane stove was empty. He took it off and screwed on a fresh one. It was the last canister they had.

I'll make some coffee, he thought, when I've cleaned the pans. He'll like a mug of coffee.

He began to clean the pans with grit from the glacis spread on a little cloth. As he started on the first one it occurred to him that he was on his own. The Czechs had gone. They had been there when they were needed. Now they were gone. The next act devolved on him. Slowly he rubbed the cloth round and round in the pan.

If it came to the worst, he thought, he would have to act alone. He felt isolated. But it was not unpleasant. Almost exhilarating. Like climbing a sensationally exposed pitch on good holds. Abstractedly his hand circled the pan as he imagined himself coping with the crisis, handling the worst that could happen (supposing he dies, he thought with sudden dread).

Then the first notes of thunder rolled through his fantasy with a long, sullen rumbling.

He put down the pan and went out on to the glacis. In the north-west a long black cloud, flat-topped like a wave, loomed over the Oberhalbstein. It was travelling east.

Daniel stared at it incredulously.

Only a few minutes earlier the sky was empty. Completely clear. He stared in astonishment at what seemed to him a shocking act of malice. Every few seconds the thunder rolled like gunfire. As he looked beyond the glacier he saw flights of birds rising and swooping down the valley towards the forest. The thunder grew more violent. Within seconds the echoes of one reverberation merged with the first rumblings of the next, while the cloud swept towards the north-east face. It moved with extraordinary speed. Daniel watched it coming as it poured unopposed over the low hills beyond Molino. He saw the lightning stab and flicker. In minutes the little Piz d'Averta, four kilometres away, was overwhelmed. He saw a gigantic, fiery lance punching into the summit cone.

It was like some dreadful apocalypse, full of horror and panic, in the beginning only partly known, now flowing back so wholly and terribly that he understood it for the first time. The rending noise in the yard. Aunt Catharine's white face. The cries of women as the labourers stove in the casks. Wine washing over the cobbles. The green and golden wine of Alsace. One old indomitable voice crying (against the crash of glass and splintering wood) 'Sois gentil! Sois fier! Sois sans peur!' as the first tank nosed into the lane.

Then the light vanished in a whirling, smothering mist.

The storm came, not with the roll and crackle of thunder, but with the violent blast of the first shell. Then the staccato clatter of hail raking the face until the great walls of the diedre were racing with a white cascade. He scrambled back from the glacis while enormous hailstones leapt and spattered in the aluminium pan. Thunder and lightning were simultaneous. A colossal crash exploded with a single flare at the mouth of the cave. Even through closed eyelids he was dazzled by the glare. For some moments he crouched against the back of the cave. Then, when awareness flickered back, he heard, as if through some appalling nightmare, a faint, familiar voice calling him to shelter. He crawled stiff-limbed into the tent.

The wind screamed after him. A sudden storm of hail spattered the tent, threatening to wrench it from the pegs. It was pitch dark. He could see nothing. His hand groped over a large boot.

'Fasten ... the door!' yelled a voice.

Obediently he turned to do as he was told. Each time he gripped the thin fabric of the sleeve it whipped back out of his hand. The whole tent rocked. He had to roll into the doorway, pinning it under his body so that he could draw the tapes fast over the sleeve. The slight lull that followed was a blessed relief.

The voice came again. Muffled, but with an obstinate insistence.

'We'll ... be ... all right!' it shouted.

Instantly, another tremendous crash shook the glacis. A sheet of flame sprang up beyond the front of the tent as if the sky had caught alight. For a few seconds the livid glare banished the darkness. Daniel caught a glimpse of Raymond propped under the back wall. The corpse-like head helmeted. The good hand clutching a cigarette. Then the light collapsed in another monstrous explosion, echoed by a vast subterranean rumbling that seemed to come from the roots of the mountain.

Daniel sank back on to the folds of his duvet. Lightning! Lightning was capable of lopping off the glacis completely. The thought appalled him. He sat up suddenly and scrambled back to the door, groping through the darkness, his hands clutching at the wildly flapping walls.

'Where ... you ... going?'

'Axes,' he shouted. 'Must ... move them.'

'No!'

The voice came back at him, muffled but with the same firm hold.

'Make ... no ... difference. If it strikes ... come down ... the dièdre.' Only then did Daniel realise that the fault must serve as lightning conductor to the upper face.

'Don't ... worry!'

The voice found a faint way through the howling wind.

'We're ... low down ... we'll ... get ... through!'

The hail kept up a continual drumming against the walls. The wind struck blows from every angle, and the little tent ripped and wrenched at its anchorage.

'Must ... unclip ... front krabs!'

'What?'

'Get ... the tent ... down!' Raymond shouted. 'It'll ... go ... otherwise.'

Daniel fumbled for the door. As he did so one corner tore loose from the guy and half the tent collapsed on top of him. He struggled against the wrappings ferociously, terrified that the tent (and they inside it) might be bundled down and over the glacis. Then his hand groped across the tape. He pulled it loose and thrust his head and shoulders out through the sleeve.

He was checked violently. He had to crawl through the entrance on his belly. The rock was soft and wet. He kept his legs inside the tent so that he could find his way back again, rolled over, and shone his torch at the front corner. The beam cut from the darkness a triangle of light through which the snow streamed in torrents. The corner of the tent was drawn taut and quivering against the wind. When he released the karabiner the fabric whipped suddenly from the beam of light. He heard a muffled shout. He swept the beam down and across the tent. It had been rolled up like a carpet. Then he began the struggle to get back inside. The tent resisted him ferociously. Eventually Raymond managed to separate the two front corners, thrusting at them with his feet, and Daniel wriggled back through the sleeve. He was exhausted.

'Hang ... on ... to the corner!'

They lay side by side, facing one another in the darkness with the loose cloth bundled up beneath their bodies, each gripping through the fabric the karabiner which held the back of the tent at his end, while the storm swept over them. How long they lay like that Daniel could not tell. He hung on grimly to the karabiner. At first his hand ached. Then it lost all sensation as the pain advanced along his forearm. When the cloth ripped loose from his fingers he realised that they were crooked in a kind of rigor, but gripped nothing. He changed hands.

From time to time a small voice shouted obstinately, as if through several layers of cloth.

'Hang … on! We'll … be … all right!'

The day wore on. Thunder crashed through the electric air. The shock of it left him quivering. In all his life he had never endured such a storm. But he hung on to the karabiner. In his terror of the lightning he tried to control it, telling himself that if he stuck to the karabiner, if he kept the tent from tearing, he would survive. He gave himself entirely to this delusion, praying for strength to cling to the karabiner. He couldn't speak to Raymond. But he listened to him. He clung to every word. He was grateful even for the craziest remarks. He was desperately afraid. But Raymond, as if deaf to all contrary opinion, with the storm at its height, maintained his obstinate judgement.

'It … can't … last,' he yelled. 'Can't … last!'

Another appalling crash shook the glacis, and another, and then a deafening whipcrack snapped through the air, followed by the most dreadful ponderous, crushing and splintering, and he was thinking *Christ*! there goes the glacis, when he was struck massively on the back of the head. Vivid sparks of fire leaped from eye to eye. There was a tremendous roaring in his ears, the roaring of flames, and he reflected with queer, fascinated horror, that his brain was burning.

He must have lost consciousness for a few seconds, for he was next aware of a loud voice. It was shouting desperately, close to his ear.

'We … must … get … away!'

It was his own voice.

He felt sick and foolish. He was trembling violently. His body jerked and quivered. His legs shook so uncontrollably that he knew Raymond, lying at his side, must feel them shaking.

'Frightened!' he yelled.

'So … am … I,' Raymond shouted. 'Lightning … worst! Lino Casaletti … had a second … killed! On the Verte! Struck down … split second!'

'I think … I've … been struck!'

'Shock waves!' Raymond shouted.

Gradually Daniel's shaking subsided. His head ached. An occasional spasm shook his limbs. But he clung grimly to his karabiner. Outside the tent the wind raged on.

He stared blankly up into the darkness. A few centimetres above his nose the roof rattled incessantly. He became aware, gradually, of a discomfort in his left shoulder. Something pressing. It was Raymond's boot. That boot, planted solidly against his body, seemed the only durable, unyielding thing in the whole rattling, flapping, shifting universe. However slender Raymond's reserves of strength, however serious his injuries, they did not seem so now. That boot offered a resistance as concentrated and unmoved as the storm was wild and violent.

Then, quite suddenly, the wind backed. It was as if a great door had been closed against it. Occasional blasts still struck the tent. The terrifying noises persisted, but muffled, further off. They could hear frozen snow drumming on the fabric. The vivid shocks of light and the sharp crackle of thunder were still violent, but distinct now, no longer simultaneous. The centre of the storm had shifted.

'I hope … the Czechs … got off!'

Even as the words were yelled Daniel heard a low, distant rumble approaching through the wild noises of the storm. It was so far off that at first he thought it might be the St Moritz express crossing the valley, but it grew so swiftly, gathered with such a terrible vibration that the solid rock …

He knew, then, what it was. He flung both arms up to protect his head and buried his face in his duvet.

The whole tent lifted. Daniel's hand was torn from the karabiner. He felt his body plunging through the fabric floor as the blast sucked out the thin sac like a paper bag. He heard a sharp cry of pain. Then he was struck violently himself in the mouth by some heavy solid object as they were tossed about in a terrifying panic of threshing arms and legs. He dug his fingers vainly through the tent floor, scrabbling for the solid rock, while Raymond clung desperately to the one remaining karabiner.

For hours the fresh snow had gathered on the icy slopes below the summit. Only a stroke of lightning, or a blast of the wind was needed to set it off. Now it had happened. The whole unstable mass was loosed, pouring off the ice like water, gathering between the funnelled walls above the hundred metre corner, bursting with a blast that could flatten a forest like a field of corn.

The whole face trembled as the great avalanche thundered down the diedre. Daniel gave up the struggle with the rock and pressed the duvet against his head to stop his ears. Huddled on the floor of the cave with his eyes closed and his head buried in the down-filled jacket, all his senses straining to shut out the avalanche. He didn't move until its last echoes had died away down the face.

Then he felt Raymond's boot prodding his arm again.

'All … right?'

The tent roof lay heavily over his head. As he pushed the cloth away from his face he felt the weight of fresh snow resisting his arm.

'All right?'

He thrust the cloth aside. There was a taste of blood in his mouth. He hadn't been aware of it before. He felt with his tongue. The lip was split. A tooth loose. Blood still seeping.

'Something … hit me,' he mumbled.

He tried to speak without moving his lips.

'What?'

'Hit … me … in … the face!' he shouted. This time it hurt.

'You'll … be … all right!' The last two syllables arrived together, as if pushed with immense effort through the almost solid air.

Now it was necessary to hang up the front guys again. Daniel undid the tapes around the entrance, but before he could get out he had to push the sleeve upward in front of him through a bank of snow. He crawled out. The darkness of the tent gave way to a grey murky light. It was bitterly cold. He stumbled, slipped through the thick powdery snow, his fingers fumbling for the front wall of the tent, feeling for the guys, clipping them back into the karabiners. It took a long time to repair the broken guy. All the while the snow piled up in wet, sticky clumps on the back and shoulders of his cagoule. It stuck fast to the tweed thighs of his breeches. It trickled between the thick fibres of his stockings. When the job was finished and he crawled back into the tent, he carried with him a large quantity of snow which oozed over his ankles between the rim of his boots and slithered down his neck to join the sweat drying coldly under the cagoule. He rolled miserably on to his *pied d'elephant* and clutched the duvet with shrunken, saturated fingers.

'Christ!' he said.

'Never mind,' said Raymond. 'Warm and wet's better than cold and dry.'

'I'm bloody cold,' said Daniel viciously, 'and bloody wet as well.'

He knew it was far from over. Lightning and the terrible wind might strike as violently again. A blizzard might rage for days at a time on a north face such as this. If that happened, he thought, we're finished. We're as good as dead already.

He lay still on the soft folds of the *pied d'elephant*, his head pillowed on the duvet, gazing sightlessly at the roof of the tent, sensing a vague wet warmth now rising from the down-filled cloth beneath his body. He thought of nothing. The long effort to hang on had exhausted him, left him with nothing in reserve to face the worst of all. We're going to die. It was as simple, as final, as that. And it was fixed in his mind. Locked there with such conviction that all his conscious efforts to take up his friend's confidence not only failed to overcome, but actually intensified his sense of death. And he had nothing left with which to ward it off. The Czechs were gone. Were dead, probably. And the storm would come again. Besides, in Raymond's confident assessments he saw a foolishness of such dimensions that it could come only from an insane determination not to recognise the facts.

He's mad, Daniel thought. Mad!

Outside, the wind howled unrelentingly.

Yet, gradually, his cold wet clothing warmed to the heat of his body. Beneath him the soft pressure of the duvet and the *pied d'elephant* offered a damp, melancholy comfort, in which the harsh noise of the storm seemed strangely pacifying, like the crooning of a savage nurse. He lay in a kind of dream, brooding on Raymond's madness, remembering his brother André, first one, then the other; images shifting, converging, merging in one composite last scene fixed like a picture in the mind. Like a cartoon by Goya. Hooded figures in a blizzard. Tiny, before the Plan's gigantic bulk. All heads but one bent to a dark bundle in the snow. Close to the snow a lantern: light flashing under the outstretched arm: gleaming on an eye, the rim of a face in shadow, one half of a bearded mouth, parted, framing the words: It's André – he's dying.'

Outside, the howling of the wind erupted from time to time in shrill flurries that drove fresh snow against the wall. The tent was stifling.

Tous les grands chefs se sont tués.

The words passed dreamily through Daniel's mind.

At the Cabane des Planches, in stained red slippers, Gaston shuffles between the tables. On the panelled walls he keeps a row of faded portraits. *Tous les grands chefs*. A long line of serious, bearded men – they began as crystal seekers, poor woodcarvers, hunters of chamois. Now they sit or stand, each in his own grave poise, like village elders, or prosperous, provincial public men: François Couttet, in middle age, descending a staircase; Old Melchior Anderegg, like Moses in a watch and chain, holding an ice axe; Jean-Antoine Carrel's remote face, turned back, perhaps to Chimborazo and Cotopaxi, years before.

Jean-Louis Belmonte calls it 'Gaston's graveyard'. They are very like the photographs the Italians put on tombstones. He takes great care of them. Often he'll pause in wiping the long wooden table by the wall and polish each glass front with the edge of a coat sleeve gripped between his fingers. Once a year, on their anniversaries, he fixes a black ribbon to each wooden frame. Oh, the young men don't care for it at all. Not at all. The guardian of the cemetery, they call him.

'*Tous les grands chefs,*' he says. '*Oui! Je les connaissais tout le monde!*'

'He couldn't have known them all,' said Belmonte, the young tiger. 'Some of that lot must have died almost a hundred years ago.'

That was true. But no one knows how old Gaston really is. You can't tell from his face. He's so old it doesn't matter. Like the survivor of an ancient race whose hold on life is to maintain this link with the famous dead. To preserve the memory of those English captains who dined off fresh trout and Château Lafite, carried up for them to the Refuge des Grands Mulets.

'There's Christian Almer,' he would say, 'the man who carried a fir tree to the summit of the Wetterhorn. And that great fellow there (pointing to Ulrich Lauener) on the Eiger glacier, when all the Chamonix men were terrified and said the séracs would crash down at the slightest sound, that fellow climbed the tallest pinnacle of ice and shrieked like the devil. Yes! Shrieked like the devil.'

Each aged countenance stares down indifferently from the wall. Only Maquignaz's hollowed, bandit's face gleams with amusement. He was killed too. *Tous les grands chefs.* Imseng, 'who had neither wife nor children and wanted none', who loved only the Macugnaga face of Monte Rosa, the great snow wall which made his name, then killed him. Johann-Josef Bennen, who trod the snow catenary on the Wetterhorn. Crossing that couloir on the Haut-de-Cry he saw the snowfield split above him, watched the crack widen, begin to slip, to slide ...

'We are all lost,' he said. '*Wir sind alle verloren!*'

He might have spoken for them all.

Tous les grands chefs se sont tués. The snow closed in to fill the places they had left.

It was snowing now. Snow muffling, deadening, burying everything till not a trace was left.

8 Chapter 8

The cold woke him. Bitter cold and cramp. A great weight of snow lay up against the tent. He put out his hand to touch the wall. It was stiff with ice. He had no idea how long he'd slept. The wind had dropped. It was pitch dark. It might be midnight, or the last hour before dawn for all he knew. Nothing moved. A profound stillness brooded over the mountain. He heard Raymond's low, deep breathing and guessed he was asleep. But his own sleep had brought him no relief from the hopelessness of their position. Except that now he felt a flicker of irritation, a faint desire to take a stand against the storm – a mood, perhaps, of the dream he'd woken from and still remembered.

Not a particularly narrow plank, he remembered. You could walk along it easily if it was just lying on the grass. Ten metres above the bottom step it was a different matter. Not many of the boys would even set foot on it. The few that dared did so as if they were treading a tightrope. Every precaution they took for their own safety seemed to increase the hazard. The outstretched arms plunged wildly, bodies dipped, swayed, as each boy lurched above the drop.

Raymond stirred in his sleep and muttered something that Daniel couldn't catch. He listened, but the disturbed moment seemed to have passed.

It was still the same plank you could walk along easily if it was lying on the grass. One knew that. That was a fact.

Yet one little boy got halfway, then dropped astride the plank, clinging to it with his arms and legs. Nothing anybody said could make him move. A crowd of boys gathered in the court below. Some of them racing up the steps, scattering the little heaps of leaves that Brother Michael had swept down from the bank.

The boy was very frightened. He was crying.

'Come on! Crawl forward!' they shouted.

'No! Come back! This end's nearer.'

'Shut your eyes!' said fat Martin.

'You fool!' they all shouted furiously. 'You'll make him fall.'

Then, quite suddenly, there was silence. You looked where everybody else was looking, to the top of the steps where Brother Jerome stood as still and as silent as a wraith. Not a sound. Only the boy's stifled little sobs.

Raymond stirred again, and called out in a sharp, protesting voice. 'No! No! Lionel!' he called.

It was strange how he always seemed to come at you silently and from above. Not like the other brothers, who might have appeared among the boys at the bottom of the steps. Not like Brother Superior, whose kind, white head seemed to precede him like a light. A sort of *lumen Christi*. No. The face staring from the window, the dark shape moving in shadow on the landing, the tall figure at the foot of the bed – that was always Brother Jerome. He turned his pale, expressionless face on the crowd of boys. They drifted silently away. He strode softly to one end of the plank and took two firm paces forward, extending a long, black arm to the little boy, whose fear of a fall was lost in the far worse fear at his fingers' end.

'Take hold!' said Brother Jerome.

The boy was hauled to safety and the plank removed. And everyone was punished.

But the trick was not to think of falling off. Or learn to think of it so dispassionately that it no longer seemed very likely. Like the man who carried the bull on his shoulders. Learn to do it in stages. That night he and Denis slipped out from supper, took the plank from the shed, set it three times in position (first at the top – then there – then high above the bottom step) and marched across it. Then they went back to Benediction.

Daniel smiled to himself in the darkness. If only Brother Jerome's long black arm could reach up here.

It was a good memory. A good thing to hold on. Suddenly he felt a surge of life inside him. An impulse to move – to feel the spring coming again – to climb in the sun on rough warm rock, with the hard move coming up.

But Raymond stirred again. Then, with a violent movement, he woke, crying aloud, struggling to sit up. Daniel leant forward and gripped his shoulder reassuringly.

'It's all right,' he said. Lie back!'

'What's the matter?'

'Nothing. It's all right.'

Raymond shuddered. His head ached. He felt cold. There was a bad taste in his mouth.

'What time is it?'

Daniel struck a match and looked at his watch.

'Two o'clock,' he said.

'God, I'm thirsty!'

'I'll make a drink.'

He could hear the wind rising again. It seemed to creep into the silent space between them.

'How much fuel have we?'

'Not much.'

'How much?'

'About two hours. Perhaps more.'

'Yes – we should eat something,' said Raymond.

Daniel pushed his head and shoulders out through the entrance. The blizzard had stopped, but the snow had piled up deeply under a thick crust of frost. The little ventilation sleeve was almost buried. He pulled it out and cleaned the frozen snow from its mouth. The night was very cold and still, except for the wind. There were no stars. Only a blurred, wheyish moon that gave no light as he looked critically up at it. He scooped a panful of snow, slid back into the tent and closed the entrance. It was difficult to cook anything in the tent. He had to sit hunched forward balancing the pan precariously on the steel rods (burning his fingers in the process) while he gripped the stove between his knees. The flame curled like a luminous blue fringe around the bottom of the pan, its light glinting on the few hard, steel things that lay about. It lit nothing else. But its steady hissing filled the tent.

As the pan grew hotter, the snow shrank at the edges. The icy water crept higher, cutting hollows in the banks of snow. The flame attacked it from beneath. From time to time a hanging cornice collapsed into the water. Daniel watched as the snow sank in the pan. He saw how it was undermined, reduced, drowned. He thought of himself here in the hollow cave, generating heat at the very centre of the snow and ice. His heart beat steadily. The blood still kept its temperature. His restless desire to do something was taking shape, growing to a purpose. Be patient, it said. Wait here till the storm exhausts itself. Then strike …

'Did I pass out again?' asked Raymond suddenly.

'What?'

'I think I fainted.'

'When?'

'Just now.'

'I don't know. You were restless. You called out Lionel's name. I thought you were dreaming about Gyalmo Chen again.'

It had been the first great postwar expedition. Something the press had taken up like a crusade, a quest for the Holy Grail of national pride. In Paris they built a monstrous wooden tower so that the more reckless citizens might imitate their heroes among the fixed ropes and pegs and wooden holds. Raymond had been profoundly shocked.

'What was it like?' asked Daniel. 'You never told me.

Raymond made no reply. He kept silent for so long Daniel thought he wasn't going to answer.

'Gangtok!' he said suddenly. 'That's where it starts. That's where you meet the porters and the yaks.'

Then he began to speak.

'From there you go north-east to a place called Kupup that means the summit of the saints. That's where the track divides. One path goes up to the

Tang-la pass, then down into Tibet. That's the ancient road from India to Lhasa – the pilgrims' road to Chomolhari. You can see it a long way off, towering up beyond the pass. And Siniolchu, and Kabru, and even Kangchenjunga, a long way off to the north-west. The air's so clear.'

'All the great names,' said Daniel softly. 'Kangchenjunga Chomolhari Lhotse … Makalu … Everest … '

'Chomo Lungma!'

'What?'

'Everest,' said Raymond. 'Its real name is Chomo Lungma. Goddess Mother of the world. That's what they call it.'

Raymond took a cigarette from the packet at his side, lit it, then lay back on the sac. The wind droned on outside the tent, but its noise was almost lost in the steady hiss of the stove. A steam was rising from the pan.

Daniel felt drowsy.

'At Kupup,' Raymond continued, 'above the road, there's a fortress carved from solid rock. Hundreds of years old. It faces north. Whatever comes from the north must pass beneath it. A great black shape against the snow. It's a grim place. The porters wouldn't camp there. A place of blood, they called it.'

He was silent for a while. The cigarette glowed in the darkness. He was a long way off. Daniel could sense that. And his voice seemed weary. But he carried on with his tale.

'We took the other path,' he said. North-west, to the Turn-la monastery. That's where you first see Gyalmo Chen. Set in a great chain of peaks, with the Rushung river hurtling through the greatest gorge in the world. You could put the Eiger in that gorge …'

Daniel thought of that with awe.

'Gyalmo Chen is the holy mountain of the Lepchas. The Great Queen, they call it. They say that the Rushung river is her gift to them. And that every spring, when the snows uncover the fir tree forest, the rhododendrons burst into flower at the touch of her feet. That's what they say.'

Daniel forgot the pan of water steaming between his knees. He listened, spellbound.

'Every colour you can think of,' said Raymond softly. 'White, yellow, mauve, red, pink. All the colours.'

His cigarette glowed again in the darkness. He blew out the smoke, and went on more briskly.

'They have a ceremony called the *parikharma*,' he said. 'A kind of pilgrimage. They have to make a circuit of the mountain. Some of them *crawl* round the whole chain, over passes of 5,000 metres or more. They have gloves tipped with metal. They lie face down, stretch out their arms and make a mark in the dust with the metal tips. Then they go to the mark, lie down, and mark the path again. And so on, right round the circuit. They eat and sleep where they lie. It takes many days. Some of them die. They acquire great merit by making that circuit. The *parikharma*, it's called.'

He stubbed out the cigarette in the little tin at his side.

'That water's ready,' he said.

'They believe everything has a guardian spirit,' he went on.

'We believe that,' said Daniel.

He took the pan off the stove and set it carefully on the floor of the tent. Then he reached for the tube of milk.

'It can only protect you against yourself. It cannot guard against the man who wishes to do you harm. Only his spirit can do that. And there are evil spirits, too. The spirit of cold – the dysentery spirit – there's even a spirit of adultery. They are disembodied and they seek to enter men. The Lepchas do not say of someone – "he is an evil man". They say "he is possessed of an evil spirit". Sometimes men give themselves. Sometimes they are taken by force. But the gods are good as well as terrible. They can protect those who love them.'

'You admired the Lepchas.' said Daniel.

He handed a mug of hot sweet milk to Raymond who sat forward to take it.

'They are good,' he said. 'They are happy. They lead simple lives of work and prayer. Whatever its superstition a religion that can accomplish that …

He stopped again and was silent for a time, sipping meditatively at his drink. Now that the stove had stopped its hiss Daniel was conscious of the wind again, driving between them, separating them.

'We stayed three days at the monastery,' Raymond went on. 'We had to break down the loads. Everything had to be carried up the gorge. I used to talk to the Abbot. "We do not ask what may exist after what exists," he said. "We follow the Way. We do it by our own strength alone."'

He paused, and drank again.

'Beyond the mountains you can see the Chinese guards patrolling the frontiers of Tibet. We saw them down in the Chumbi valley, a long way off. We saw the glint of their bayonets in the pass. If they cross the border the Lepchas will resist. No one will help them. Not us, not their gods, no one.'

'They will not blame their gods for that,' said Daniel.

'No!' said Raymond. 'I don't suppose they will.'

He finished his drink and handed the mug back to Daniel.

'"We are all bound upon the wheel of things. Lives ascending … descending … far from deliverance." That is what they will say.'

Daniel did not understand about the wheel, and the lives. But he detected the note of bitterness and kept a sympathetic silence for a while, sipping at his lukewarm milk, until his child's desire to hear the story's end broke out again.

'Go on!' he said. 'You entered the gorge?'

'Oh, yes! We had to. There's no other way.'

Raymond was hesitant now, his voice faltering from time to time.

'It's the greatest gorge in the world,' he went on. 'Two thousand metres deep. You could put the Eiger in it – and at the bottom the Rushung river racing between the walls. Nothing can live in it. There's no path. Sometimes you're high up on the wall – sometimes stepping from boulder to boulder in the riverbed. And there is something more. Something hard to describe. A kind of dread. The porters felt it more than us. We felt it perhaps because they did. Perhaps it had to do with the noise. Not just the usual river noise. But something behind it, like a much greater noise a long way off. Like,' he hesitated, 'say, an avalanche in the great central couloir … '

In the dark Daniel nodded.

'It never stopped. The further we went the louder it grew. And we knew that if we lost a single porter the rest would turn back. We had to fix ropes for them. Three times we had to cross the river on bridges we made ourselves. After four days we came out of it, into a kind of basin filled with fir trees. Everything was soaking wet. And the noise – everyone shouting – the roar of water …

He paused, lit a cigarette, then he continued.

'Beyond the trees was a kind of inner amphitheatre. Great walls hundreds of metres high, with the Rushung river crashing down from a great slot in the rock.'

'You got through?' said Daniel.

'We got through. André found a way up the cliff to the upper gorge. We followed. We got the porters up somehow. Then we went on. For two more days. Sometimes by the water, sometimes high on the walls. Fixing ropes, crossing and recrossing the river, the porters swaying under the loads and chanting prayers as they went. God knows what they thought of it all. Then, quite suddenly, round about noon on the sixth day, it was over. We passed beyond the walls.'

He stopped again.

'What we saw– ' he began and hesitated.

'Yes?'

'So many things … I can't really describe … '

Yet it poured out – as bewildering as it must have seemed to him all those years before.

'Beneath the snowline,' he said, 'a great meadow. Flowers and butterflies, hundreds of butterflies. So many things, I cannot tell you. A great stillness. A softness of the air. Ferns – orchids – butterflies – so many things. Among the rocks there were sheep that had no fear of us at all. So tame you could touch them. You could stroke them with your hand. Greenness and colour everywhere … '

Daniel was silent. He remembered a green valley near Allos, not far from Mont Pellat, in the little alps of Provence.

'And at the head of the valley – the holy mountain. Towers – great battlements of ice – glaciers like white channels against the grass. And so dazzling you couldn't bear to look. Surely the gods dwell here, the Lepchas said. Tsung-ling, they named it – the garden of the great lady. We must have been the first men ever to set foot in it.'

He drew for the last time on his cigarette, then stubbed it out.

'So we rested there for a while. Set up the base camp, prepared loads for the higher camps, and so on. Then we began. Up the main glacier, through the ice falls. Past sécracs as big as churches, some of them. Day after day. And everything went like a dream. We pitched the last camp at 7,000 metres, in a small saddle on the arête. Lionel, Andre, Pasang Tendi and I. The wind was bad all night. Lionel was sick. He and Pasang should have gone for the top. He'd dreamed of it for years.'

Daniel nodded. He knew of Lionel's dream.

'We wanted it for him very much. But he was sick. He just wasn't up to it. So at dawn Pasang said, "I will care for him: the sahibs must finish it."'

He stopped. For some time now his voice had sounded faint and faltering. This time he was silent for so long that Daniel began to wonder uneasily if he had passed out again (it was so dark he could see nothing) and was about to enquire, when the tired voice began again.

'He gave me his *khata* – that's the white scarf they have (Daniel nodded) – to place close to the summit I put it with the Abbot's prayer flag. Then we set off, André and I. It was snowing. Pasang watched us go. We turned round at the top of the slope. He was still standing there. Outside the tent. We waved. Then the mist swirled up.'

He paused. In the silence that fell between them Daniel caught a sense of all the lonely places of the earth – and of the courage that men bring there, like gifts for the gods.

'All the way up it snowed. We came to this big rock step in the ridge. I led it. Suddenly – I was in sunlight. We were there. Great peaks all around us. Kabru, Kangchenjunga, Chomolhari, Simvu, Siniolchu; they were all there. All glittering in the sun. I couldn't get over that. The sun! And we were there too. And there was the summit. Just a few more metres up the slope.'

'Yes!' Daniel said suddenly. 'I remember! You had to stop short of the summit.'

'It seemed so silly,' Raymond said, reflectively. 'So silly to stop like that. To have come all that way. Not to get up it properly.'

'You made a promise. It was right to respect it. To respect their gods.'

'Yes! We made a promise. We gave our word. I gave my word. I told them all that we stopped short of the last few metres.'

Raymond paused.

'That was a lie,' he said.

'It seemed so silly, then,' he went on. 'No harm could come of it. No one would ever know.'

But *you* would know, thought Daniel.

'Besides, it seemed wrong not to do it properly. Wrong to us. To ourselves. So we went on. We drove our axes into the summit We took photographs. We even flew our flag from the top.'

At last he stopped.

Daniel floundered for words to fill the silence.

'Photographs?' he said. 'Surely … '

'No!' said Raymond. 'We took those from below the summit. There were others that no one saw. Two. André had one. I have the other. I have it here.'

He reached behind him with his good hand. The movement must have hurt him for he gasped with pain. Yet he managed to unzip the little pocket in the top of his climbing sac, took out his wallet and tossed it across.

'It's in there,' he said.

It was too dark for Daniel to see. He had to switch on the torch. The photograph was in a little cellophane packet. He took it out. It felt cold and slippery between his fingers. He shone the torch and stared at it. He saw a black shape against a brilliant sky. A hooded, muffled figure. Ice axe held aloft in the familiar attitude. Teeth a white flash in the masked face. Under the padded boots steel teeth gripped the snow.

'It doesn't look like you,' he said.

'No,' said Raymond. 'It's the altitude. The ultraviolet light or something. The goggles don't help.'

Daniel held the photograph unhappily. He couldn't think of anything to say. Silently he tucked it back in its wrapper, replaced it in the wallet and handed it back.

'We'd brought some things to put in the snow,' Raymond went on. 'Some chocolate. Pasang's *kharta*. A crucifix. The Abbot's prayer flag. We buried them like thieves … ' The flat voice shook a little but kept its course. 'The gifts of simple men to the gods, and we buried them like thieves. Then we went down. And of course there was the blizzard. You know about that.'

The whole of France knew about it. Daniel kept a sympathetic silence.

'Snow avalanching all the time,' said Raymond softly. 'Goggles choked with snow. It took hours to get down. Hours. Looking for a tent that wasn't there anymore. There was nothing. Only fresh snow. Oh, we looked for them. Christ knows we spent hours searching … shouting … probing in the snow … But they were dead. They must have been swept straight down the south-east face. They were dead.'

He fell silent, and Daniel pondered on the agony of that night. Caught without shelter at 7,000 metres, with one's friends dead. At least he'd been spared that. He was thankful he'd not had to suffer that.

'You've never been back,' he said, 'have you?'

'We had come a long way,' said Raymond, after a pause, 'through difficult country. All that way, with so much effort, for' (he hesitated) 'a violation. That's what it was. For something that can never be put right.'

For the pride of a moment, Daniel thought.

'You didn't realise … ' he began.

'No!' said the leader firmly. 'That's what it was. An outrage. And two men gave their lives for that.'

That's what shakes him so, thought Daniel. That Lionel would not have done a thing like that. Never. And yet who knows? Who can tell?

'It was a long time ago,' he said consolingly. 'It's all in the past now. What's done's done!'

'Men are defined by what they do.'

'Men are worth more than that,' said Daniel sharply. 'Besides, we have all done these things. I have done these things.'

'Then you will pay for them.'

Not for the first time Daniel felt a profound regret for all men who have no gods to pray to for forgiveness.

'You can go back,' he said impulsively. 'I'll go with you. Next year we'll go back. You and I together …'

It was a foolish, desperate idea.

'No!' said Raymond. 'I shall never go back.'

Daniel's slim resources were exhausted. He could think of nothing else to say.

'There have been other things since then,' he said weakly. 'Yes! A brother left on the Plan … '

'That was not your fault,' Daniel broke in harshly. He'd been through this before. 'André was strong. He was experienced. He was a professional. You couldn't have known what would happen. Besides, you had other duties. You had a client.'

'I had a brother, too.'

There was nothing left to be said.

Each man withdrew. It was like leaving the field of another indecisive battle. There was a space between them, a no man's land, dead ground filled by the wind which drove fresh snow against the tent.

There you have it, Daniel told himself. Bitterly, he remembered his foolish pride of the previous morning – that he could replace Tomas – that things would be all right after all. Recalling it now was painful and embarrassing. But perhaps a little of it did him credit. It was up to him. That bit was right, anyway. Except that the conditions were different now. They'd changed. And he did not really believe he was up to it. Even if the Czechs had reached the top, and the storm lifted, a rescue on the face would be difficult and dangerous. He couldn't be sure that the Czechs had got to the top. The chances were that they had not. He had to face that now.

Then he realised that he had been trying to face it all day. Ever since the lightning started. Not until now had he been able to do so. To go beyond the fact. To face its consequences.

'Some things' (put in a sombre voice) 'are forbidden, even here.'

'Forbidden?' Daniel wasn't really listening any more.

'Not by God,' said Raymond. 'I mean, simply, that we ought not to do them. It is as if they were forbidden.'

Daniel felt for a reply, hesitated, then let it drop. If the Czechs were dead it would be two more days before Lino raised the alarm at the Masino hut – that is, if Lino got there on time. He might not.

Suddenly, at the thought of Lino's homely face, his cheerful greeting, he was filled with anguish.

'What I mean,' said Raymond, 'is that there are some things that I cannot permit myself to do.'

'I don't see how you can say that,' Daniel said, suddenly irritated. 'I don't see how you can say that you do not permit yourself to do a thing when it is precisely that thing which you have done.'

'No – I make laws for myself,' Raymond insisted. 'I may do things which break them from time to time, but they are still things which I forbid myself.'

'Then you must forgive yourself,' Daniel said sharply. 'No one can do that.'

Daniel grunted. Food for one more day, he thought – if they were careful. And one cartridge of gas – already started. 'No one can do that.'

'What?'

'Forgive himself.'

'Then you must live with it.'

Immediately the words were out he was sorry. Shocked that his own hopelessness should come so easily between them. He didn't want that.

'Look,' he said consolingly. 'Forbidding – permitting – what does it all mean, really? Language is like a kind of searchlight. At a certain altitude it fails. It doesn't work anymore. The light keeps travelling out but it's too weak to light up anything clearly any more. They trusted you. They asked you for a promise. Out of respect you gave it. And then broke it. That is what it amounts to. A betrayal, perhaps, but still a human act. Something we all do. Something I have done. None of us are guiltless.'

Raymond made no reply. In the silence and stillness the low murmur of the wind caught Daniel's ear, a confidential ide whispering discreetly, lest he forget the most important thing of all. The weather might lift. It might not. If it didn't, and they stayed where they were too long, they were as good as dead already. Nothing was certain, nothing was sure, but that. That if no one came to help them they would die. And since he could not be sure that anyone would come to help them, Daniel concluded bitterly that they must help themselves: bitterly, because he had never expected Raymond to be injured, or the storm to break so suddenly upon them, and because he wished things might be otherwise. But these things had happened. He had come on this adventure, and he must try to bear its consequences as best he could. He would do what he could. He did not really expect to succeed.

'Tomorrow,' he said, 'we must go for the top.'

Raymond made no reply.

'We can't stay here,' Daniel added. 'We have no food. We don't even know whether the Czechs … '

'Look.' Painfully, Raymond raised a shoulder from the ground. 'If you fell …'

'I know that,' said Daniel. 'Do you think I don't know that?'

For some moments they were silent again. They heard the wind howling over the wastes of the north face. To Daniel it seemed an elemental voice confirming the decision.

'We have to go,' he said. 'Don't we?'

'Yes!' said Raymond.

Daniel realised that he had been wrong in thinking his life a preparation for something that never happened. It was happening now. For both of them this moment had always been out there ahead, awaiting their arrival. A destination to which they had to come.

Yes! Carried with us, thought Daniel. Like his photograph. Like the cheap toys in my sac. Like the letter I shall never finish now.

And he was not ready. He was not prepared at all. Oh, the good life wasted. Wasted! Years of dreadful waste!

Now the years behind seemed like a tragic misappropriation. Lies. Promises betrayed. A brother dead. A man reduced by years of argument. A woman's voice that spoke now only to itself … exhausted … at two o'clock in the morning ('and I thought I would get myself a little dog … ').

'We must be mad!' Daniel said. 'You and I, we must be mad! All the lovely things in the world. All the lovely things, and we come to this God-forsaken place. We must be mad!'

He raised his left arm, the arm which bore on its underside his father's watch ticking against the pulse, and smashed it down against the rocky floor. The glass splintered. The little hands broke off.

For a moment he remained stock still, too stunned by his own impulse to realise what he'd done, or to feel the pain in his wrist.

Then he raised the watch to his head. In the silence its creaky ticking filled his ear.

Part 2

9 Chapter 9

At night, at that altitude, nothing stirs. Nor can any sound carry.

The face lay under a bitter frost that always comes with the last hour before dawn. Only Raymond's breathing broke the silence. Harsh and rapid, it rose and fell ... rose and fell.

He had passed out again. Perhaps he was just sleeping. Daniel didn't know. Too cold and wet to sleep for more than a few minutes at a time, he was wide awake now. His breath issued in puffs of watery vapour that turned to ice at the tent wall. His lips were cracked and sore. His loose tooth hurt. There was a bad taste in his mouth.

As he listened to his friend's breathing he wondered how *he* would face his fourth day on the wall. The man was crippled. How could he climb? Not without aid. He might not climb at all. Yet he'd survived half a dozen crises almost as desperate. But for him six men instead of four would have died that day on the Plan. Perhaps he was still stunned. Still confused. But when – if – he recovered he would think of nothing but escape. That formidable will would not desert him.

For a moment Daniel felt the weight of that granite obduracy – that prodigious instinct for survival. And since Raymond was crippled, *his* arms would have to wield the axe and hammer, his fingers clutch at the ice, and there would be no relenting, no letting go until he'd suffered all the stations of collapse.

To rope straight down the wall was quite impossible. But time and time again during this last hour before dawn his mind slipped in imagination down the vast expanse of the central face: the grey rock slipping past, his body sliding nearer ... nearer the ground, to the last bound out across the bergschrund, to the crunch of boots on the glacier, to the moment when he could pack up and go home. But each time he stopped short. If only there were three of them. It might be possible to lower an injured man – but he was checked again. Stopped. Forced back to the worn circle of doubts, hazards, fears, decisions made on insufficient information, equipment selected or abandoned, ropes and pegs to be fixed, trusted, and all of it now based on the bitter recognition that the Czechs were dead, that above him stood 600 metres of vertical rock, verglassed, the cracks sealed with ice, the chimneys choked with rotten snow and rubble.

From time to time images of his wife and child slipped through his mind. And, momentarily, he held them there, considering the faces that stared remotely back at him. But they were too far off to matter anymore. He had been three days and nights on the face. His friends were dead. His companion crippled. Filthy, wet, reduced to a physical squalor he could never tolerate at home, he had experienced a severing from all the objects of a clean, well-ordered life. Storm and avalanche had accustomed him to an icy world where nothing lived for long. And these privations weren't without effect: they attacked the comfortable casing of his mind, bared it to absence, darkness, death. Now, unprotected, it compacted to a single obdurate purpose. It was the only tenable purpose in a wilderness where men maintained themselves so brutishly and with such pitiful provision that the least chance could kill them. He was determined to get off. Cold, motionless, swaddled in the sodden clothing, he watched and waited for the dawn.

At first light he went out, floundering on hands and knees through the deep drifts until he could get out on to the glacis beyond the cave. The raw air stung his face. A bitter chill settled about his body. But after hours of crouching or lying in the muggy tent it was a relief to stand straight again. He was astonished at the great weight of snow which covered the rock. The rubble that had littered the surface two days before was blotted out. Here and there boulders or blocks of ice loomed up like shapes under a thick blanket, but the rest was obscured beneath a dense white sheet that slipped down to the mist. There was nothing to be seen. The village, the valley, the spires and turrets of the Zoccone spur, the glacier, even the upper lip of the great roof had vanished in the freezing fog.

It hovered like a ghostly wall around the face. Constantly it drifted in trailing strands wherever the eddies of the wind disturbed it, coating everything it brushed against with a thin film of frost. Ice materialised on Daniel's beard and eyebrows. His cagoule crackled as he walked.

Shivering, hunched in the soaking duvet, he trudged about the snow, peering up at the huge buttresses that hung like islands in the cloud. From time to time he stopped and looked to the north-west. There was Molino. It was strange to think that there were men asleep down there below the cloud. Families asleep, or waking, in houses whose roofs would shortly catch the first rays of the sun. He wondered if ever they looked up from their streets or pastures to see clouds trailing across the face, and if ever they thought what he always thought at such a sight – behind those clouds perhaps men are fighting for their lives. It was the same impulse that, at nightfall, made men like him pull on their boots again, take up ropes and axes and go out on to the glacier. He thought of the first rescue he'd ever been on. He could remember only bits of it. The speed of the guides; his fear of not being able to keep up; the white, frightened face turning and turning as the stretcher jolted over the snow. He did not doubt that beyond Molino, in the valleys, villages and little towns of half a dozen countries there were men who would do as much for him. But for all that mattered now he might have been standing on another planet. The sun which shone for other men did not shine here. Now it must not shine at all. If, at the next midday, the sun shone above the summit the fresh snow would avalanche. Darkness and cold were vital. If he prayed for anything he must pray for that.

At last he turned away from the fog and plodded up the glacis, stumbling as the snow crust broke and slid back under his boot. Once or twice he slipped and felt a clutch of panic lest he should not recover but slide on down over the edge of the great roof. When he got back Raymond was still asleep – or unconscious. Daniel tied up the sleeve to make a small, open circle in the tent wall. He crouched down on his haunches at the entrance. The flimsy roof, heavy with snow, pressed down on the back of his head, icy cold at first, then wet with water drops that trickled down his neck. He rummaged in the big sac and produced a bulky canvas bag which he placed on the floor. He unfastened the drawstring and then drew out into the faint grey light the lobster-clawed, twelve-pointed Grivel crampons.

They were his own crampons. He removed the rubber cover that guarded the points and tested each one against his thumb. All sharp. He always kept them sharp. He lifted the first by its thin steel frame and placed it lightly on the snow. There it rested, poised on its points above the fragile crust: skeletal, motionless, its lobster claws held in a steely, warlike posture. He placed the other on the snow beside its mate.

There were only four cigarettes left in his packet. He lit one now, resolving to smoke no more than half of it. He took the north wall hammer, the climbing dagger, the top half of the demountable ice axe and his own small piton hammer and tossed them out on to the snow. He felt calm and empty. Many men had been in far worse situations and survived. Here on the glacis the snow was rotten. He thought it would be different higher up. Driven by the fierce wind, forced under pressure into the cracks and chimneys, it should compact into a thin, hard layer. The crystals would break down. Meltwater and the bitter frost would turn them into ice.

He picked up the ice axe and held it loosely in his right hand, flicking it from side to side with a practised movement of the wrist. It wasn't his. Even cut in half like this it didn't suit him. He put it back inside the tent. When he'd finished half his cigarette he squeezed out the end between his thumb and finger. He would have to smoke them all in halves. He would reward himself with one whenever he'd done something hard. Of course it would be patchy. There would be stretches that gave way. But in the cracks and chimneys, supported by the rock, it must surely hold.

Wherever there is snow, he remembered – it was a saying of the old guides – *there one can go.*

He clutched at this now.

The ice dagger and the two hammers lay there on the ground in front of him. His own hammer had dropped head first in the snow. The steel claw of the pick slanted up towards him, thick and rigid against the snow.

As he looked at them his mind turned back to Mont Blanc years before. To the great ice trinity of the Brenva Face. The Pear Buttress, the *Sentinel*, the *Route Major*. He thought of snow flashing past under the long glissade again. *The Verte, the Blaitière*, the *Forbes Arête* on the Chardonnet; one long glorious summer.

At dusk, on the days he wasn't climbing, sometimes he used to stand within the little square of tents counting the dots that moved slowly over the Vallée Blanche (four ... five ... six – black against the snow) then, happy his friends were safely home again, he knelt to light the stove.

He shook his head. A summer that had been a state of grace.

He put out his hand and took up the dagger in his fist. It was no more than a thin ice piton, bound at the head with tape. He made a few, swift stabbing passes, weighing the long, light peg against the solid curve of the pick. It seemed as flimsy as a paper knife. He put it back in the sac.

Snow changed, he thought. Temperature and stress were never constant. He had to climb straight up, on the four front points alone, belaying from whatever pegs the rock would take. For two days at least he would have to live and work beneath the vast unstable load of the summit snowfield – with no protection – upon a surface that might collapse at any second. And if he fell ...

'What time is it?'

Raymond's voice was weary but awake, as if he'd lain for a long time not sleeping but with eyes closed against the light.

'Time we made a move.'

Raymond hauled himself upright with his good hand and struggled clumsily to push the *pied d'elephant* down over his hips.

'Here,' said Daniel. 'Let me do it.'

They cleared the tent as quickly as they could. Daniel passed things out. Raymond took them and tossed them on to the snow. When the tent was empty Daniel crawled out through the entrance. He surveyed the jumble of clothes, equipment and personal belongings strewn about the snow. The little chamois lay upside down, its carved white belly exposed between its stumpy legs. Anguish clutched at him again for a moment, but he shook it off. He had to shake off that. He picked up the wooden toy. One of the horns had broken off. He brushed the snow from its head and tossed it into the open sac.

'Can you manage to pack up?'

Raymond nodded.

They worked steadily without speaking. It was bitterly cold. The raw mist still hovered at the edge of the glacis. There was no sound except for the clink and thud of equipment, and the scuffle of boots in the snow. From time to time, scarcely distinguishable in the grey air, a few flakes drifted down. Eventually, when everything was done, Daniel looked around at the neat pile of equipment, and at the bare place in the snow where the little orange tent had stood. He gazed at the ice-fringed face of his gloved and hooded companion, dried blood clotting the beard and hair, and felt for a moment such an emptiness that he was overwhelmed.

He shuddered violently.

Raymond looked enquiringly at him but Daniel only shook his head.

'We'd better go now,' he said.

They tied on to one half of the doubled rope, leaving fifty metres free for Raymond who would climb it with the help of tapes and prusik clips. Daniel arranged a chest harness to keep him close to the rope as he climbed up it. That should keep him from falling backwards, Daniel thought. He should be all right with that.

'Can you manage these things with one hand?' he asked. He meant the prusik clips.

'I shall have to.'

Daniel knelt to strap the crampons to his boots. His fingers were cold and clumsy, and it took him a long time to thread the straps and fasten the buckles. He clipped the two hammers and one end of the rappel rope to his waist loop.

Raymond helped him on with the climbing sac, looped the slings and the piton carrier over his shoulder and handed him his helmet silently. Daniel put it on. He raised his hand to fasten the strap beneath his chin.

He could no longer see the great hanging buttresses that guarded the upper face. The main wall stood silently within its covering of cloud. From its centre the snow-filled crack of the *direttissima* rose and receded into the drifting mist. The wind was rising again. Flakes of snow which twenty minutes earlier had drifted singly and intermittently now drove down in short, spasmodic flurries. Daniel looked about the frozen desolation of the glacis, and at the bare spot in the cave and was prepared to take a long farewell of its pitiful security. But the soft pressure of ropes and straps, and the stealthy clink of steel whenever he moved, oppressed him. He was ready to go. Yet he hesitated and looked doubtfully at his companion.

'Do you think you'll be able to manage?' he asked.

'I'll have to. Let's get on with it.'

The crack was fairly wide, and though he couldn't trust the thin layer of frozen snow which plastered the back wall (it broke away too frequently), he found sufficient holds among the small ledges and seams on either side. But it took a long time. Most of the crack was glazed with ice, and he was so aware of his profound responsibility, so certain of the consequences of a fall, that each placing of a single crampon point exacted the utmost caution.

So he went on. Working tightly, his instincts like voices in his ear: Take care. Don't fall. Do not exhaust yourself.

Yet there were other voices warning with equal force of the dangers of delay, of the effects of hunger and cold, of gradual exhaustion. And the urgency of all this was heightened now by the visible grimness of the face, isolated within its iron wall of cloud, cut off not only from the rich, warm colours of the forest and valley, but also from the comforting sight of life.

From time to time he came across new pegs driven into the crack. But they were no use to him. And the Czechs were gone. No voices broke the silence of the face. Only his own harsh breathing, the creaking of ropes, the chip – chip – chip of his own hammer pecking at the ice. His was the only human presence. His noise the only purposeful noise. This thought gripped him so powerfully that on one occasion he stopped still and listened. Nothing stirred except the wind. Behind him the ropes creaked softly. He thought of Sedlmayer and Mehringer creeping up the great icefields of the Eigerwand – slower and slower until storm and exhaustion stopped them altogether – of poor Longhi's cries: 'Fa – a – ame! Fr – e – ddo!' drawn out on the wind.

But the mild character of the crack persisted. After much patience and caution he ended a long run-out of almost fifty metres at a stance set like a saint's niche in the fault. It was snowing steadily now. He couldn't see Raymond. He could see nothing but the grey rock, curtailed by cloud, and the coloured ropes dropping down into the mist. He cleared the snow and ice from two new pegs driven into the top of the niche. They were Jaro's pegs. He clipped the rappel line to one of them, tied back the red rope to the other and leant out to shout instructions down through the cloud, straining to catch the indistinct replies that climbed back up to him. Then he began the arduous recovery of the sac, hauling it hand over hand through the karabiner above his head. The fingers he'd burnt on the stove the day before began to throb painfully as the thin line cut into his glove. When the sac was secured he removed the rappel rope. He tied back to the karabiner the white rope up which Raymond would climb on his tapes and prusik clips. He ran the red rope through a second karabiner clipped to the first, and when he was satisfied with his preparations he leant out again over the void.

'When you're ready,' he shouted.

He took up the red rope again. His hand was hurting badly, and it needed an effort of will for him to grip the rope firmly. But he'd begun to have doubts about the chest harness arrangement. The mechanics might not work. He thought of Raymond sliding the clips up with one hand, stepping into the swaying tapes, fighting to stay upright. He mustn't fall backwards. Each time the taut rope yielded he took in the slack swiftly and kept it tight. He leant far out over the drop, ignoring the pain in his hand and the numbness of his feet, straining his eyes to pick out the dark shape looming up through the cloud and falling snow. He was desperately concerned to bring him safely to the stance.

But this anxiety only sharpened his awareness of delay. It was all taking too long. Far too long. As the snow piled between his feet he felt the great weight of rock that separated them from the summit, the hundreds of metres still to be climbed. He lived through pitch after pitch of this slow, agonising crawl up the rope.

Several times the movement stopped altogether. He assumed Raymond had passed out again, and gripped the rope grimly, determined to hang on to him, no matter how long it took.

But supposing he dies, he thought. Supposing he's dead now.

Gradually this anguish undermined his courage. As the slow minutes passed so the conviction grew in him that in a few hours' time they would simply peter out miserably somewhere on the upper face. When, at last, Raymond materialised through the shifting gloom Daniel brought him carefully up to the peg, but said nothing. Nothing sufficed to break the bitter silence in his mind.

Raymond spoke cheerfully.

'*Simple!*' he said. 'There's nothing to it.'

But his face was grey and exhausted. His clothes were plastered with snow. He sank into the crack below the stance while his companion unclipped the white rope.

'Here!' said Daniel. 'You forgot these.'

He handed down the prusik clips and tapes.

Then it began to snow in earnest. Daniel was determined to reach the shelter of the great overhanging buttresses in one long run-out if he could. The wind tore at the ropes ceaselessly. He could feel them snatching at his body. From time to time he shrank against the rock as little falls of fresh snow burst down the face. As the crack deepened, in its approach to the buttresses, he thrust himself further into it to escape the wind. Then he found it difficult to see the moves clearly. The falls of snow increased. He began to curse himself at his own rising panic. But he struggled on; and had just reached Jaro's peg at the mouth of the first chimney when he heard Raymond's voice shaken out in long syllables on the wind.

'We … can't … go … on!'

Daniel knew it.

Bitterly he drew in the eighty-metre rappel rope, clipped it to the peg, and began the descent.

Just before midday they were back on the glacis.

Wearily they set about clearing the fresh snow from the cave. For Daniel especially it was a bitter setback. He felt himself the victim of a terrible unfairness at the heart of things. He had climbed well, with great determination. Now they were back again. They had achieved nothing. And their small store of energy had been reduced still further. It was as if the delicate structure of resistance that had begun to grow on the wall that morning had been summarily chopped down. And though he expected such a reaction in himself, although he knew that all men would suffer the same in such circumstances, this knowledge was powerless to hold back the dreadful sense of futility which crept through the mind like a paralysis. Deep down some instinct still flickered its desperate message to whatever pockets of resistance might remain. We must get off! We must get away! But there was no response.

All the while the wind drove fiercely at the glacis raising the fresh snow in great powdery clouds which fell on the floor of the cave. As they scraped the rock clear so the snow drove in to cover it again. Daniel regarded its presence with a perverse satisfaction, as if it offered an ironic confirmation of his despair. But Raymond, despite his handicap, worked away grimly, shovelling the snow aside with clumsy, scythe-like sweeps of the axe.

'At least it keeps you warm,' he said, gasping, swaying in the snow.

Daniel made no reply.

Eventually they clipped the tent to the pegs. Daniel had to hold out the front wall like a canopy over the cave until Raymond had cleared as much snow as he could. Then he crawled inside, pulled the big sac to the entrance and struggled to get the stove, the food container and the down-filled bags in through the flapping folds of fabric. At last Daniel crawled in after him and tied up the sleeve. They huddled together, shivering and exhausted, while the storm drove once more over the face. For a long time they lay without speaking, hearing only the wind and the fresh snow drumming on the tent wall.

'We couldn't have gone on,' said Raymond, at last.

Daniel didn't answer.

'It would have been crazy.'

'I know!'

'In those chimneys … '

'It's all right,' said Daniel. 'I'm not denying it. I'm not arguing.'

Raymond fell silent again. He thought of the blizzard at this moment sweeping the great slabs of the upper face, of fresh snow avalanching down the chimneys, of Daniel striving to find the right route, in failing light, with 300 metres between them and the next bivouac at the foot of the corner. Here in the cave, at least for the time being, they were safe again.

He was very sorry this had happened. Not for himself. For him (sooner or later) it was almost inevitable. Not that he would ever yield willingly, not even to the inevitable. He would always fight for life. He would cower away in any hole or corner if it gave him a chance of life. But after the Plan disaster he had no illusions. For a few more years he had lived facing the mountains – had seen the snowfields sparkling high up the great faces, felt at his fingers' ends the rough warm rock. And he was grateful for that. But he knew how the circumstances that determined André's death could reduce the very best of men: strength, judgement, skill dwindling slowly, hour by hour, to the same dark bundle, crumpled in the snow.

But most of the men who came to climb with him had unfinished business to return to. Children to fear for. Wives to love. Parents to protect. They could not afford to die. None of them could live as free as he had lived since André's death. For his freedom seemed to flourish only in loneliness – at the far side of negation.

He wished very much he had not brought Daniel with him. He knew that he had suffered the same loneliness on the face that morning. He knew what he was suffering now, and thought, with pity, of what the next day must bring.

'I thought you were mad,' Daniel said suddenly. 'Last night I was quite sure you were mad.'

Raymond stared at him.

'I suppose I was very frightened. I didn't see how anyone in their right mind could not be as frightened as I was.'

'That's because you're only an amateur. If you were a professional it would have been different. You learn to accept these things. Oh, you might be frightened. But fear – lightning – stonefall – they're all a part of it. In the nature of things.'

They were silent for a while. Daniel listened to the wind's noise and the steady drumming of frozen snow on the fabric. He saw how blanched and bloodless Raymond's face looked in the dim, orange light.

'And death?'

'That too.'

'I couldn't look at things like that,' said Daniel. 'Not in a million years.'

'One has to. In the long run, anyway.'

'I don't!' said Daniel.

Raymond shook out the cigarettes in his last packet of Celtique.

'That's what I said,' he replied quietly. 'You're not a professional.'

He had eight left. It would not have occurred to him to save them, or smoke them in halves. He would smoke one whenever he wanted one. When they were gone he would do without.

'Well, whatever you think of amateurs,' said Daniel, 'if you're to get off this face you'll need me to lead it for you.'

'If you're to lead it,' replied Raymond, 'you'll need me to tell you how.'

He offered one of his cigarettes. Daniel took it silently and struck a match for them both.

Worlds apart, he thought.

It made him think of his marriage. Of their condition. That was the sacramental part of it, he supposed. Their dependency. Their need of one another. She, of him; he, of her. Yet it wasn't all. Each of them wanted something more.

Something, he pondered, that in being beyond the other, was beyond them both. What it was he didn't know. He remembered her in the aftermath of some appalling scene. Sitting wretchedly together in the hours after midnight. Her voice. Her words, falling into the exhausted air.

'I only want to be happy. I can't help wanting that.'

And his own bitter response.

'I wanted to be a child for ever.'

For he'd believed he was right. Convinced that he'd acted as any man would act.

That was years ago. The rows were fiercer now. They went on longer, as if they'd both acquired stamina, as if time had made them tougher.

We are not fully human, he thought. Most of the time we live below the human level. And yet he knew that ultimately, when all savagery was spent (when neither had anything left to fight for) she could be reduced to the same, simple admission. And so could he.

'I only want to be happy. I can't help wanting that.'

So there are moments that restore us to humanity. Sometimes, in the aftermath of anger and violence he would feel profound sorrow – a profound pity and love for things. That was a rescue, in its way. A moment of grace. Again he saw the red-rimmed eyes in rings of blurred mascara. Streaks of black staining the swollen cheeks. All those small vanities. They seemed infinitely pathetic now.

Suddenly, he was filled with an overflowing love and pity or her. For them both. For himself too. For all of them. He wanted to put right what had gone wrong. But there was nothing he could do. Nothing. And if he was useless in this respect, then everything was useless. It was all part of the great disaster.

'Sometimes,' he said, 'I think I would like simply to be. Not to be anything … or have to do anything … Simply to be. To be free.'

'That wouldn't do you any good,' said Raymond sombrely.

'No,' said Daniel. 'There's nothing remarkable about me; I'm not a Parisian – or a Marseillais – or a native of any famous, fashionable city. I'm not noted for wit or shrewdness or courage. I am not mean. I am not one of the persecuted I am not any kind of refugee. I was born close to the border. Lived all my life there. Where the lines of demarcation have never been beyond dispute. Where even the language is unsettled. Not a good place to grow up. To learn what one's supposed to do.'

There was a silence between them. A strained silence.

With Daniel's voice hanging at the edge of hysteria.

'I have never,' he declared emphatically, 'never stood a chance of doing anything as well as I would have liked.'

This time Raymond spoke.

'Perhaps tomorrow,' he said, 'you will have that opportunity.'

It was a chilling remark. And he knew it. He crushed out his cigarette in the little tin he used as an ashtray.

'Look,' he said gently. 'You rest. Sleep for a while if you can. I feel a lot better.'

It was true: he hadn't fainted for some time. 'I'll get us something to eat.'

He began his preparations for the meal with that phlegmatic indifference to both injury and the storm that was characteristic of his extraordinary adaptability. It would take a chain of quite extraordinary disasters ever to wear his life away. Yet he knew that it could happen. And this knowledge informed his capacity for endurance with great patience, and the cunning never to offer more resistance than was necessary to survive. He moved now, softly and deliberately, collecting neither more nor less snow than it required to yield just under half a litre, lighting the stove, setting the flame to the right height, laying out the tins and bar of concentrated food. He worked very quietly.

But Daniel could not sleep. He lay with open eyes, hard up against the back wall, his head turned towards the rock. The wet fabric of the tent lay across his face. It was like an icy skin. He listened to the steady hiss of the stove until its slender noise at last pierced like a needle through the great heaving of the storm. Then he closed his eyes.

For a long time he heard his friend's stealthy movements about the tent. He thought again of the snow subsiding in the pan, of the little flame maintaining its steady, insistent purpose right here at the heart of the storm. It was like a counter movement, taking shape in secret, behind closed doors. And he realised that Raymond was far from mad. He was a *grand chef* in a dreadful game. A grand master effecting expert nullifying moves. And the encounters endless. Endless. Daniel saw him squatting perpetually on some north wall, enduring the storms and terrors of the great faces, a contemptuous eye cocked at his malignant gods. You cannot starve me, he would say to them, more than I've always starved – nor cause me greater pain than I've always suffered – nor make me any lonelier. And there he would preside for ever.

Like an antique hero, thought Daniel. Chained to the rock. Waiting for the eagles to return.

Christ! Some of us are born in hell, he thought. In hell we live and move and have our being.

In his distress he cast about his mind for some other image – a consoling presence.

Hail holy queen, mother of mercy, he began silently, covering his face, pressing his fingers against his face, *hail, our life our sweetness and our hope.*

But the images that came were desolating. A child's face. Aunt Catharine's white face. Then the dead, dreadful countenance he'd seen as a child in pictures of the Holy Shroud. He remembered his grandmother dead – they tried to keep him out but he slipped in after they had gone – lying with the sheet drawn up to the neck, her face bound with a cloth. Implacable, that face. He bent and kissed its brow, but that was not what he'd come for. He had come to look at death. He came away, shuddering.

A blankness came over his mind. Empty. Like the sky he used to gaze at as a child. Vast over the flat brown fields.

Look to the south, Uncle Paul used to say. Look to the south – one day you'll see them. The long line of slender bodies. Slender necks and bills thrust forward to the north.

It was spring again. And they were flying home.

This memory, in the midst of despair and exhaustion, gave hope of better things. Next year, he told himself, I shan't climb. We'll go to Norway. Camp in the Opland. Fish for trout. Swim. Walk in the forests. Maybe we shall see the great cranes, too.

Raymond bent over the precariously balanced stove and stirred with a cautious hand the disintegrating lumps of meat and vegetable. The pan slipped suddenly. He caught it with a spear-like thrust of the spoon and slid it back. A musty, disagreeable odour rose from the pan.

He sniffed, and thought, Christ! I hope it wasn't the snow we peed in.

He peered at it dubiously. It has a high calorific content, he told himself. It saves lives.

'OK,' he said. 'It's nearly ready. You can pour the wine.'

But Daniel was far away among the rocks and forests of the Jotunheim, dreaming of the fair, young son – of the blind, unwitting god who killed him – of Valhalla, in Gladsheim, where the heroes feasted – where all wounds were healed.

'I have a suspicion,' Raymond added, 'that we may have peed in this stew.'

But Daniel was dreaming of wolves at night in the forest – and of the great cranes dancing by the lake.

'Here you are then,' said Raymond finally. 'Whatever it tastes like remember it has a high calorific value. That might help to get it down.'

He passed a pan to Daniel who bent forward to take it. He was hungry. He ate swiftly, spooning the stew into his mouth, filled with a wild excitement. It was a revelation. It was an act of grace that would absolve him from the past. When I get back, he promised, things will be different.

'What's it taste like to you?' Raymond chewed doubtfully at his first mouthful, the spoon below his lips.

Daniel scraped the last stringy fragments of meat from the side of the pan, his mind filled with an eager, impatient joy to begin.

I'll write to her, he told himself. I'll do it now.

He cast the empty pan and spoon aside.

But he didn't write. It was still snowing fiercely. The wind kept driving fresh snow into the front wall until the fabric bulged under the great weight. The film of water vapour, which had clung in drops to the inner side above the rising heat of the stove, froze to a thick, uneven layer of ice. They seemed to be sinking into an icy gloom. It was too dark to write. And the batteries of the little lamp were almost drained.

For a long time they lay together side by side in the darkness. When they had to urinate they did so crouching uncomfortably above their parted knees, with a helmet gripped between the thighs – Daniel held it for his friend – praying it wouldn't overflow, cursing when it did, passing the slopping bowl awkwardly out through the entrance.

If this were a film, Daniel thought, we would die in the end. But we are real. We have responsibilities. Our friends are waiting. I do not intend to die. And since he couldn't write to his wife he tried to think of her as she had been in all the happy moments …

He remembered her as she'd appeared one windy day, coming over a ridge in the Vosges, a long way off. A small figure under an enormous sky, in a blue anorak that was too big. He and the child set out to meet her at the head of the valley, and when they'd reached the place he'd sat on a boulder, his eyes fixed on the col, watching, hoping she'd had good weather, while the boy played among the rocks. He found a frog, Daniel remembered. She walked with her arms held by her sides, bowed under the unfamiliar sac. The scree clattered as she came down it, stumbling in the little boots she wore. Handmade Italian boots he'd brought from Montebelluna. Her hair all blown back by the wind.

'Why do you have to climb?' she asked once. 'Why not be happy just to walk in the hills?'

But he had looked out from the doorway of his tent. He saw the black pine forests on the hillside across the valley, and above it the huge *ballon* of the summit dome, washed pink and a dark, misty blue. A late buzzard wheeled high up in the sky, gliding in slow, wide circles, hung almost still (hunting for rabbits, he thought: he heard its plaintive, mewing call, thin and urgent, like a kitten's).

He thought of her now. At home – waiting – not knowing from one day to the next – hoping, perhaps, he might turn in at any moment at the lane gate, dropping the big sac from his shoulder, tired, dirty, burnt dark by the sun.

Suddenly he was overwhelmed by an intense desire for his home. His eyes filled with tears.

Long after nightfall the storm raged on, until the tent was almost buried, and the atmosphere inside foul and stifling. They were so crushed together they could scarcely move. As the hours passed they suffered agonies of cramp. Daniel particularly suffered from the lack of air. It created a raging thirst which he tried to slake by gnawing pellets of frozen snow. But this only inflamed the sores on his cracked lips and made his mouth burn worse than ever. They finished the remaining biscuits and ate a handful each of raisins, but eating hurt Daniel's mouth and intensified his thirst. The air was so foul they dared not light the stove to melt water for a drink. And they'd need what was left of the fuel to cook the last bar of concentrated food. They spoke seldom. From time to time one of them muttered something – speaking offered some relief from the oppressive, stifling atmosphere but for the most part they endured their ordeal in silence, as though each wished to conceal from the other his growing sense of hopelessness.

Time passed wearily. Raymond bore it dourly, scarcely moving, lying there as if he had put up the shutters and bars and was prepared to sit out the winter if necessary. But Daniel took it badly. He felt that he had been compelled to take part in a dreadful game, under terrifying rules, where the least infringement met with death. And then, when he was going well, he had been swept back to the start. Now he must begin again. Only this time it would be harder. There was no hope of moving before dawn. They had many hours to wait for that. Second by second, as each hour added fresh snow to the face their chances were slipping away. As he lay there listening to the storm he knew that he was present, watching and waiting, at the gradual extinguishing of life.

In all his life he'd never known anything like this. He had never even imagined anything like this.

Now he realised that the worst of life had always been like this. That always it must be like this for someone, somewhere. And perhaps the time had come for him to suffer what all men must have suffered since the beginning.

Imperceptibly in the darkness his lips moved through petitions he had used since childhood. But all the time he knew that if he opened his eyes he would see the tent looming in front of his face. That he had only to lift his fingers a few inches to feel the ice thickening on the fabric.

For the wind moved constantly. The little insistent sounds began again. The creak of frozen fabric, the soft scurrying patter of snow, like children late at night, demanding, demanding, until he came up wearily to the question they had both avoided.

'What sort of chance do we have?'

'Every chance,' said Raymond swiftly.

'I would prefer to know what you think.'

Raymond hesitated. He was no longer sure about himself. He'd fainted again, though he hadn't told Daniel. Another day and night at the glacis might very well finish them. Yet, even if they made a start at dawn the next day, they would have no chance of reaching the summit without another bivouac on the face. They had to survive at least another forty hours, if not more, with one meal left and perhaps just enough fuel to cook it. It wasn't enough. Above them were almost 500 metres of rock and ice that would extend a strong man, climbing protected, in good weather. And Daniel had to face it alone, in appalling conditions, after four days' exposure on the face. Perhaps a man has a right to know where he stands, Raymond thought, so that he may do with dignity whatever has to be done.

But he could not bring himself to say it directly.

'Very well,' he said. 'I am not a religious man, like you. If I were I suppose I would pray.'

He paused. Daniel listened to the soft scurrying of the wind against the fabric. It reminded him of rats – rats in the barn at home.

'Though what you would expect to get from it,' Raymond added bitterly, 'I can't imagine. A fiery chariot would come in handy.'

'I have been praying,' Daniel said with dignity. 'Though I expect nothing. And I hope for no more than you. A change in the weather. Firm ice higher up. Enough strength.'

He thought of her coming over the ridge again alone, stumbling down the scree – the wind piling clouds above the col – yes, between the boulders the little boy had found a frog.

'You're a queer sort of Catholic,' said Raymond.

Daniel saw her coming out from the great boulders – beginning to run clumsily, her hair streaming out – and the child ran towards her – and he ran too, and so they were all running and laughing and calling to one another.

He smiled and shook his head. 'You do not understand,' he said.

'No,' agreed Raymond. 'I understand only the tangible things that happen. The rock I stand on. The things that threaten to dislodge me.'

All three of them had met with a stupendous collision of bodies – arms flung out, gasping for breath – and he fell backwards, laughing, and they all collapsed on the grass …

'On the great faces,' Raymond added, 'that's all there is men, and rock and ice.'

'Does nothing ever shake your certainty of that?' asked Daniel curiously.

'Nothing. Except,' he hesitated, 'oddly enough … perhaps ... sometimes … music.'

Daniel was astonished. The idea was so extraordinary.

'Sometimes, I find myself supposing that the music is out there, in infinity, with no beginning and no end … as if,' he hesitated again, 'as if someone had brought back just a few moments of something that is going on for ever. It's my fancy, of course.'

That there should be these depths, Daniel thought. Even in the unlikeliest lives.

'It began with something I once heard a long time ago,' Raymond said. 'I've never heard it since. Perhaps I will, one day.'

For a long while Daniel was silent.

'That tune,' he asked eventually. 'How did it go?'

'There was a tune, I suppose,' replied Raymond. 'But nothing I could hum or whistle. It was so complex … so intricate. It seemed simply to exist. You know? It simply *was*.'

'Yes,' said Daniel doubtfully. 'I think so. I've heard tunes like that.'

He pulled the hood down over his eyes, drew in the sleeves of the duvet, and hugged his arms across his chest. He huddled close to his companion. The cold was venomous. But that night it had been so hot they made a bed upon the grass and made love there, and drank Calvados and watched the stars. He showed her the Plough and the Little Bear, and Scorpio, with its great red star.

An icy chill settled on his loins. It spread slowly across his back. The floor was hard, but he lay motionless. He was too miserable to move. But in the soft hollow of her belly that night the light had gathered like a luminous pool. Her skin gleaming like limestone in the darkness. He pressed his hand there, uncoiling his fingers in the moist hair, pushing them into the warm wet division of flesh until she reached out and drew him on to her. He felt her breast against his mouth – the salt, sour taste of her – and all night long the child had slept without stirring.

But Raymond did not sleep. He felt no pain, apart from the discomfort of cramp and the ache of stiffened limbs. He was tired, but he couldn't sleep. He lay awake hour after hour, silent and unmoving, lost in a fog of gloomy thoughts that thickened as the night wore on.

Men die every day, he told himself.

But not the men who occupied his mind: they died on the seventeenth of August. Andre, in silence, surrounded by comrades – poor Guerin, suffering agonies of fear – Maillot, alone, roped to the ledge where they'd been forced to leave him – René Lebadier – even Varaud was dead now: killed in the Pamirs. He alone survived.

He was not a superstitious man. But he had lived all his life in a valley where myths are precious, where old men's tales persist, and are remembered even by those who disbelieve in them. Now the familiar legend flooded back as potently as the names and faces of the men who perished. Alberico. Borgna. The great Ottoz and his companions, caught and swept away. Even Morra, Schiavi's old comrade. All killed on the seventeenth.

One day's as good as another, he thought. Dying or being born.

But this was still the one day above all. He said no prayers. He did not go to mass. But it was his own festival of the dead, and he kept it, just the same.

At length the wind dropped. If the snow still fell, it fell silently. No light of any kind penetrated the icy fabric of the tent. Through the close dark silence he heard the sound of steady breathing, regular and soft.

He's asleep, he thought. And he was glad. For the second time that day a generous pity welled within him. And a profound regret. He has no business here, he thought. A pious, domestic man who went to mass on Sundays with his family – he had no business here. Then he remembered that Daniel chose to climb – that he couldn't be entirely domestic, nor his piety sufficient – that he had *chosen* to put himself at risk in a place where all things were permitted.

We are alike in that, he thought. And yet he has no business here. He has better things to do.

For some time this phrase fixed itself painfully, and accusingly in his mind. *He has better things to do*.

But suddenly a thought leaped within him like a revelation, and the phrase vanished, eclipsed in a flash.

He's good on ice!

It was true. Really good. Small … light … moved carefully …

If the ice was hard, if he had enough strength …

But these were questions that could not be answered now. The consequences of the weather, of the changes of temperature, the possible consolidation of snow and ice, these things marshalled themselves before him like factors in a complex intricate puzzle. And he was too tired to cope with it. His eyes closed. He was close to sleep. Yet his mind hung on to the persistent expectation (more belief than expectation less belief than hope) that they might still get off.

He lay quietly for a long time, emptied at last of despair and hope alike, waiting for sleep. And just before it came it seemed to him that he could hear Bach's discordant horns, the *corni di caccia*, blowing faintly through the darkness.

10 Chapter 10

Pain woke Daniel. Like a tiny coal glowing and fading in his stomach.

For a few hours he had slept uneasily, twisting from side to side as the pain grew more insistent until a sharper spasm woke him. He groaned and opened his eyes. It was dawn again. The air was thick and foul.

He lay there drowsily for a long time, only half awake, bracing himself whenever the pain flared inside him, engulfed in the malodorous atmosphere. But it was dawn again, like a fact demanding his acknowledgement, and so at last he opened the sleeve and crawled out into the frosty air.

Thick fresh snow covered the glacis. There were no footprints, no marks of any kind. Not a trace of their activity remained. The wall of freezing fog stood exactly as it had twenty-four hours earlier. Nothing had changed.

He relieved himself sluggishly in the snow, shivering as the cold air struck his thighs.

She has always asked what happened, he thought. I do not know. In the beginning we understood nothing. We only wanted to be happy. We could not help wanting that. It was out there in front of us. Like a door on the horizon. Closed, but ours. It would open only to us. It seemed fixed there for ever, as if time had petrified, and we passed together along the road saying to ourselves, 'when we get there it will be grand! It will be marvellous!' But we never got there. Perhaps we never moved at all.

He fastened his climbing breeches and trudged back to the tent.

We felt things happening, he thought, but did not understand them. Growing older. Getting dressed each morning. Taking off our clothes at night. Trying to stay human. Failing mostly.

We have spent our lives, he thought, waiting for something that never happened.

But the pain, at least, was better now. He crouched at the entrance, reached inside and rummaged with one hand in the big sac.

Perhaps this was his disability. This radical dissatisfaction. An infirmity he was born with. To aspire continually. Always to fail.

His fingers groped over the edge of the little flat biscuit tin. He took it out. On the lid, once, had been a picture of a girl in peasant dress, smiling, offering a basket filled with honey cakes. At her ear a swarm of bees curled back to their row of hives in an orchard.

Yet there must be something else. An existence free from dread and self-disgust. Loving. Being loved. In a state of joy before all things. It could not be talked about. It could not be put into words. It was like a possibility that never chanced to happen. An alternative route that no one ever took.

The tin was scratched and battered now. The orchard and the bees were gone. And the girl's face was disfigured. No trace of a smile remained. Except in his memory, at the corner of the scratched mouth, in the mild eyes.

He opened the tin. On top lay a few postcards. Alpine views, of a kind sent home to friends by tourists. The top one caught his eye. He stared at it for a moment (a pretty meadow – soft grasses, larkspur, blue gentian; the great face of the Dru where two of his friends had died, serene as a cathedral) then put the cards aside. He took out his wallet, his passport, and the squirrel badge from Cortina he'd bought for the child. A notebook lay at the bottom of the tin. As he picked it up the empty, unused envelope dropped out from the leaves. He put the cards, his wallet, his passport and the badge back in the tin and laid the envelope on top. It was still clean and fresh, addressed in his small, neat hand, and stamped with a Swiss stamp. He took up the pen from the tin lid and opened the notebook. The blank, white page confronted him. He knew that he had to write something. But he didn't know what to say. For a long time he stared at the empty sheet of paper, nursing his need to write, striving to protect it from the hopelessness of saying anything that mattered any more.

He didn't know what time it was. His watch was broken. It ticked still but the hands were broken off.

So he wrote:

Dawn.
17 August.
N.F. Piz Molino.
In the cave above the great roof.
I cannot write much. It is almost time for us to go. We have been four nights on the face. There was an accident. Raymond is hurt. We met two friends but they are dead now. They died in the storm two days ago. The weather is still very bad. If we get off I shall not climb again. Not like this. Next year ...

He was about to tell her about Norway when it struck him. It no longer mattered. How was she to get this? If he got of the face the moment would have passed. His letter, its message of need, the explanations he had hoped to give, would slip into the debris of the past, would lie in the junkyard of events that could not be revoked, nor felt, even, exactly as they were. Not remembering, he would be ashamed.

And if he died ...

Either way it no longer mattered. He felt utterly impotent, gripped by events, crushed in the agonising vice of things happening. He thought of the pitiful bundle of effects that they would send her. In his anguish he shook his head helplessly from side to side. Postcards … clothes … pegs … wedges … Strange bits of metal whose names she wouldn't even know. That she should look at them and think – he used these … cleaned them … kept them carefully …

His heart burst at the thought.

Filled with terror at what was coming, agonised at the emptiness of what had been, he took up the envelope, turning it so that he should no longer see what he had written beneath the stamp, and tore it in pieces. He couldn't scatter them on the snow. At last he thrust them into his pocket and left them there.

But the letter remained. Unfinished. Spoilt. Done with. He could add nothing to it now. Gently he detached it from the book. Yet, as he read it through he realised that the words were too recent, too close to his own need, for him to stifle them completely. The desperate moment of loneliness was there on the page in front of him. He could not ignore it. He could not disown his own dependence.

At last, he thought, I know what it feels like to be myself.

He noticed, low down on the wall at his side, a horizontal flake overlapping the solid rock. He took his wallet out of the tin and removed the photograph and the few francs that remained of his money.

On a strip of cotton sewn into the leather hem she had stitched his name. He gripped it between his thumb and finger. His hand was so cold he couldn't feel it there, but he gripped it and tore it out. He put the photograph and the money back in the tin. Then he folded the letter carefully, slipped it inside the flap of the wallet, and thrust it down into the flake.

It's over, he thought. It's all over now.

He reached inside the sleeve and shook Raymond vigorously.

'Come on,' Daniel shouted. 'Let's get on with it!'

But he kept his face out of the tent so that Raymond should not see him crying.

The snow was very bad. The little cracks and seams he'd found the previous day had disappeared. Again and again, for metres at a time, the fault was choked with rotten snow. In such conditions the small hammers were useless and he had to use the ice axe, chopping with the adze held half an arm's length above his head. The snow collapsed on top of him like thick, wet flour. At first, at each of these obstructions, he was terrified lest he should chop down a solid block that might knock him from his steps. But he learnt quickly to carve the snow in pieces so that most of it passed between him and the rock. Behind the snow was hard ice and for a time he was almost happy, chipping expert nicks for his gloved hands and his crampon points. He worked hard.

Before long he was wet to the skin, yet he did not feel the cold. He kept moving. But it all took time. Almost an hour to reach the saint's niche. Almost as long again to bring up Raymond, who passed out again and had to be held for several minutes. Yet, when he began on the long run-out to the overhanging buttresses, the consequences of delay no longer troubled him. Time did not seem to matter anymore.

It's all over now, anyway, he thought. We'll go on, he thought, until we can go no further and then we'll stop.

The past no longer mattered. He was not climbing for tomorrow, or the next day any more. Only for the present, for each move as he made it. And as he moved up the long approach to the buttresses he began an obscure, private celebration of his own technique. He took pains to do all things well. Every blow of the axe, each subtle, shifting pressure of hand or steel point done for its own sake.

Gradually he passed beyond sight of his companion. The mist closed in between them. He was alone. He stopped to listen, but the face was silent. There was no wind, no creak of ropes, nothing. He could see nothing but the mist and the snow-plastered rock.

He listened again. Absolute silence. He looked at the great, grey walls of granite that flanked him as far as he could see at the little granite knobs, fixed in ice, beneath his fingers, at the cracks and wrinkles seamed with hard ice. He felt the solidity of all objects that offered him resistance, that shut him out from themselves. Nothing in the world would melt to receive him. He was alone.

He climbed on. He never thought how far he had to go to the buttresses. He made each move as it came. The axe swung into the snow, swung back, swung in again, swung back (reversed mechanically in the hand), chipped at the ice, swung back, chipped again. The splinters glowed like fire on his face.

If he fell, he died. He knew that. No one saw him. No one heard him. If he chose to stop now no one would know. But for the moment he chose to climb, climbing unaided, unprotected, climbing alone, climbing for himself, balanced on steel points and fingers, poised and alive because he willed it, and performed it.

At that moment, as he looked upward, he saw a dark mass take shape and thicken behind the mist above his head. Within minutes he had pulled himself up between the icy walls that split the great buttresses. When he was wedged there at the open mouth of the chimney, when he had fixed pegs and clipped in slings, and when he looked down at the two ropes dropping … disappearing below the vague grey mass that cut him off from the sight of his companion, from sight of the earth below, from any sight of life, he knew he wasn't ready.

He looked down at the steel points of his crampons gripping the icy walls, and the ropes dropping through the mist, dropping down to where Raymond waited for his call.

'Come on!' he shouted.

He took the red rope into his hands on each side of the karabiner and gripped it firmly.

'Come on! I've got you.'

But when he saw that powerful body dragging itself out of the mist – the grey, drawn face turned up towards him, he was profoundly shocked.

'I'm OK,' Raymond gasped.

He looked dreadful. His lips were colourless, his beard and eyebrows glazed with ice. Ice clung in fragments to the corners of his mouth. Only the eyes lived in a dead face fringed with ice.

'I feel better than I look,' he muttered.

He wedged himself into the chimney below Daniel and sank back against the wall. His head drooped momentarily over his broken arm, but he made an effort and kept it upright.

'Is it very bad? If so … ' began Daniel.

'No! No! I'm OK. Let's get on with it.'

There was good hard ice in the chimneys and very little snow. They were set deep in the buttresses, one above the other, with a horizontal scoop and a wide platform like an eagle's nest separating them at twenty metres. He stopped there, brought up Raymond and then moved on into the second chimney.

The walls were narrow and enclosing, but he did not find the climbing difficult. He was small and the ice made his progress much less strenuous than it might have been had the rock been clean. He could climb here, as he had hoped, almost entirely on the crampon points, and he went fast. It was dark in the chimney. The walls enveloped him securely. He felt the solid pressure of his body, of his back and legs against the solid rock. He kicked the steel teeth of his boots backwards and forwards accurately, precisely. At every move the good, hard ice secured him.

But all the way he was uneasy. Time had begun again. Time, the nature of the face, Raymond's condition … they began to press heavily upon his mind. He became conscious of the dull pain in his hand and mouth. Pain gnawed intermittently inside his stomach. And now the mist was swirling in the upper reaches of the chimney. He raised his head to watch it pouring silently down between the walls. It thinned hung – reformed – thinned again, and through it he glimpsed the side walls opening, falling back. He lowered his head, pressed his hands against the wall behind him, raised his body and began again wearily kicking the points into the ice. In a few minutes he reached the top.

He wedged himself uncomfortably across the chimney. A rough projection of rock or ice dug into his back, but he disregarded it and looked out over the edge. As far as he could see, receding in the mist on either side, the great boiler plates of slab that formed the roof of the buttresses debouched into the upper face. Huge. Steep. Sheathed in ice. Broken only here, at the chimney mouth, where the shallow groove of the *direttissima* began. It was choked with snow.

And he thought, I'm not big enough, or strong enough, or good enough for this.

He knew that somehow or other he had to get out of the chimney and into some kind of stance in the groove above. But he couldn't see how to do it without aid. The pressure in his back began to hurt. He put both hands on the wall, raised his body slightly, and looked down.

It was Jaro's peg.

They had got this far, at least.

He thought of Jaro driving in that peg, and knew, instantaneously, that there must be another piton above him in the groove. It made all the difference. Unhurriedly now, he clipped an ether to the peg, reversed his position cautiously, climbed up and, with one boot braced on the wall behind him, swung his axe into the snow.

He found the piton at the second blow.

Raymond arrived just as the first flakes of snow began to fall.

'We're going well,' he said.

He looked like death. Even in the chimney, with his body weight supported by the walls, he had taken almost an hour to make less than forty metres. Yet he fought to get into the étriers. Then he squatted, eyes closed, his head thrown back. One by one the snowflakes settled on his face. His sound arm hung down against the rock.

Daniel looked at him and thought of the 100-metre corner somewhere in the mist above their heads.

'If it's bad we could stop here – or go down to the ledge …'

'No!' said Raymond sharply.

His eyes opened. He shook the snow from his face. If they stopped now, they might stop for good. He knew that.

'No!' he repeated. 'We must go on.'

'But can you make it?'

'Yes!' said Raymond. 'I can make it. We must go on.'

As Daniel turned to begin the next pitch the mist swirled aside and for a few seconds over a hundred metres of the face was visible. Daniel saw great, grey walls curving backwards to infinity, and the *direttissima* like a long white ribbon, glittering with points of ice. But he could not see the corner. He did not know what time it was. He could not tell how many hours of daylight remained. There was no way of telling.

All that could be known for certain was revealed in these few seconds. The corner, and the bivouac at its foot, was hours away. The upper face began with a pitch of the sixth grade, and between this pitch and the corner there were no caves, or holes, or ledges, or any kind of shelter where they might spend the night. Then the mist rolled back again. But it was enough. In those few seconds Daniel finally understood the only terms on which he could expect to live.

Three metres up the pitch of six he fell for the first time. Jaro's peg, and what was left of Raymond's strength, held him. He had expected it. The whole section looked rotten.

'I don't like this,' he'd shouted. 'I'm putting on a runner.'

Even as he spoke the words he knew –

I'm going to fall – he won't hold me – he can't hold me –

'I've got you!' Raymond shouted.

At first he thought he'd broken his elbow. A most terrible pain flashed along his arm. Without thinking, without caring for the pain, he fought desperately to get back on the rock, fought to get up into the groove again, but when he reached the point from which he'd fallen he realised that the whole of his lower arm, from his elbow to his fingertips, was numb. He could feel nothing. His leg began to smart. He looked down. His red Cortina stocking was torn from the ankle to halfway up his calf. Blood oozed from the wound, mingling with scraps of wool. He looked up into the mist, staring up at the corner he couldn't see, and looked down again at Raymond.

'What's the point?' he said, simply.

'Look!' said Raymond. 'Just concentrate on this pitch. That's all.'

'That isn't all,' said Daniel.

'It is!' Raymond said, fiercely. 'Never mind what's up there. What you've got to think about is what's in front of you. Just the next few moves.'

Daniel saw the fierce, desperate intensity of the eyes that glared up at him from that grey, snow-plastered face. He turned back silently to the rock.

Ordinarily he might have climbed the groove by wedging or bridging, perhaps, with his hands jammed in the crack, or even by laying back against the sharp edge. But it was packed with blocks of half-consolidated, half-frozen snow, solid only in patches and held in place by weight alone like a wall of uncemented bricks. It was no more than a shaft of rubble. When he prodded it with his ice axe a strip two metres long collapsed in chunks the size of fishbowls and crashed down past the chimney.

'For Christ's sake,' yelled Raymond.

He climbed past the rotten section bridged on the icy, outer edges of the groove with his weight so badly distributed that at every move he thought he must come off. After a few metres he was so frightened that he made a desperate step across the groove and climbed up on to the slabs above the buttresses. He rested there, poised on the four front points, his hands on the hammer heads, each pick piercing the ice.

On rock as steep and featureless as this the sensation of exposure is fearful. The ice he stood on was little more than a thick verglas laid down on the smooth surface of the slab. He could see no chance of putting in a peg here, nor any likelihood of a peg until he reached the junction with the vertical face. He peered up into the mist. He tried despairingly to visualise what he'd seen during the few seconds when the mist had parted. He guessed that the slabs must go on for at least thirty metres. The thought of it appalled him. There was no alternative. He knew that if he stayed poised like this for much longer he'd start shaking. He'd come off.

The thing to do, he told himself, is to keep moving. But he couldn't bring himself to move.

Balance climbing, he told himself – three points of contact with the ice, but moving all the time. Flow up it, he told himself.

'Keep moving!' Raymond shouted suddenly. 'If you keep moving you'll be all right.'

Silently, Daniel said a prayer. He disengaged his right boot, raised it, kicked the points into the ice, raised his left arm still clutching the hammerhead, dug the pick into the ice, and stepped up. He kept moving.

But the terrible exposure, the fearful insecurity of moving over such a surface at such an angle, was overpowering. After seven or eight metres his nerve had worn down to the point of failure.

He stopped.

He peered over his right shoulder, over the edge of the slab, into the groove at his side. It looked dreadful. But higher up, slightly above the level of his head and in the centre of the groove, he caught sight of a thin strip of red against the snow. And all around it there was a curious depression in the surface, like the hollow in the snow above a concealed crevasse.

He stared at it intently: thick as a cord – and bent – like a strip of perlon …

'Christ!' he said aloud. 'It's a sling!'

He jerked the pick out of the ice so suddenly he almost toppled backwards, recovered, grasped the north wall hammer by its spike, and slowly, without bending sideways, keeping all his weight above the crampon points, stretched it towards the sling.

It wouldn't reach.

He began to lean. His right boot clattered off the ice. He swung fractionally, checked himself with his left hand straining down on the other hammer, and drew back.

'Christ!' he muttered.

He bent his head forward against the ice. He was sweating.

'What the hell are you pissing about at?' yelled Raymond.

Sweat froze on Daniel's face. He knew he would begin to shake at any second. He was terrified.

For Christ's sake! he pleaded with himself. For Christ's sake!

But he didn't shake. Slowly, with extreme caution, he traversed upward to the very edge of the slab, paused, lowered his right leg, and with the ankle fully flexed drove all ten points into the ice that lined the side of the groove. He hooked the sling towards him with the tip of the hammer.

It jerked – and held. He put his weight, gently … gently …

Still it held.

Cautiously he stepped across on to the hollow snow bed in the centre of the groove and, with one hammer–hooked in the sling, chipped delicately at the snow around it with the other.

He took a full minute to uncover the wedge that Jaro had placed in the crack. And when he found it he knew there must be other wedges. He clipped into the sling.

'Look out for yourself,' he shouted. 'I'm going to clear this snow!'

Then, leaning back on the sling, with feet braced firmly against the unstable slope of the snow hollow, and fearful of the worst, he swung the adze up and attacked the snow. It splintered and crashed past him in frozen lumps. The splinters stung his face. Showers of snow filled his mouth and eyes, and he shouted exultantly, as he drove the axe: 'We're not bloody done for yet!'

There were wedges all the way up to the main wall.

But the wind rose again as he started on the wall, driving flurries against the face. And there were no more pegs or wedges. Only hard ice in the crack, ice coating the little holds at the edge of the wall. And he went more and more slowly, struggling against the ice, and the wind, and the cold, heavy weariness that was spreading along his arms and legs. And all the while the snow fell more heavily, whirling around him as the wind grew worse.

And he thought: we have climbed this far on Jaro's pegs – now he is dead – they must have died somewhere below me.

Now that he had passed the point of their deaths he didn't know how much further he could go on his own.

From time to time he slipped into fantasies of a rescue as he climbed, only to wake sharply and angrily, telling himself that this was all useless. Their friends were dead. No one could help them. They would die alone.

But when, a few minutes later, he found Tomas' red woollen hat he couldn't bring himself to face their deaths. It was caught fast in the crack, fixed on a rock splinter, and frozen in. He freed it with a few blows of the hammer and tried vainly to brush the particles of ice from off the wool.

We will meet at the Masino hut, he told himself. We will have a big party – old Lino, and perhaps Sepp, and maybe even Jean-Louis – and I will give this stupid hat back to him.

And he stowed it away carefully inside his duvet. It was frozen stiff. Its chill struck through him like a lump of ice upon his breast.

He kept going for a bit … for a few minutes longer … for a few more metres of rock … But the sight of that red hat had broken him. The spirit that had sprung up in the groove when he attacked the rotten snow and flickered intermittently for hours since, guttered and went out. At six o'clock, at a point seventy metres above the slabs and still more than a hundred metres from the foot of the corner, he turned and looked down at his companion, slumped in the slings below him.

'I can't go on,' he said.

For a moment Raymond made no reply. He knew that the makeshift bivouac at the foot of the corner was hours away. His face, now, was almost totally concealed behind a mask of snow and ice. As he raised it to study the wall a dozen different considerations passed through his mind. He was expert in extreme situations. He knew that Daniel was far from finished. Neither was *he* finished. Not yet, anyway. He'd passed out once or twice, but he was still going. Still going. On the other hand the light was bad. And it was snowing. And as far as he knew there was nothing that would pass for a bivouac between here and the corner. For a tired man struggling in failing light on steep, ice-covered rock a fall was always likely. And the thought of a fall, somewhere up there on the vertical face, was decisive. No. They could not expect to go much further.

But they could not stop here.

Above his head, and a stride or so away, a jutting lip of rock the width of a boot rose steeply, like a stair rail, to the left in a diagonal line from the dièdre. It must be the false line taken by Schiavi. At about thirty metres it passed beneath a horizontal scoop and disappeared into the mist. Raymond looked at it. He thought of the *Fissure Lépiney* on the Aiguille du Peigne.

It was a natural ladder.

'I can't go on,' Daniel repeated. 'I'm sorry.'

'Can't means won't,' said Raymond automatically. He was still studying the fissure.

There was snow in the scoop. It was difficult to see it clearly. It kept shifting in the mist. He stared at it intently. Gradually it came to rest. A substantial patch of white against the grey rock, solid under the drifting mist.

'There's a ledge up there,' he said. 'Look! Up there to the left.'

Daniel bent backwards from the crack and peered up, craning his neck to see the fissure and the ledge. He studied them for a long time, in silence. And Raymond waited patiently. He knew what had to be done. If they were lucky they might survive another night on that ledge. He would settle for that. And he knew Daniel would settle for it, too.

'Will it go?' asked Daniel suddenly.

'Yes!'

'If you come off you'll make a hell of a pendulum across the wall … '

'I won't come off,' said Raymond.

Daniel shrugged. If he passed out again? Christ! What did it matter anyway? 'OK,' he said.

At five minutes past six Daniel stepped on to the lip of the fissure, cleared the snow and cut his first step in the ice.

The snow layer wasn't very thick. Although the lip was steep he could have kicked his way straight up the ice, balanced, with his hands pushing sideways against the vertical wall. But Raymond had no crampons. So, at every move, Daniel cleared the snow and chipped a step into the ice. He was forced to cut left-handed, with his arm close to his body, chipping at the ice with cautious flicks of his wrist, terrified of swinging out of balance. Every few metres he stopped to drive a peg behind the lip of the fissure, and clipped in the red rope. He also had to drive the pegs left-handed. He hit at them ineptly, with clumsy lunges of the hammer. Sometimes he missed and struck the wall. All the while the snow fell steadily, filling the steps he'd cut.

It grew darker. The fissure seemed endless. His wrist ached from cutting. His right hand grew numb from contact with the icy wall. But he kept going – cutting – pegging – moving almost in a dream, remembering how he and Denis would climb the stairs at school on the steep smooth strip of wood that ran along the bottom of the banister outside the rail: there was a strip missing at the top – God, what a long step up it needed, and a tug on the rail that you thought might break just then – just at that point: and Denis had become a priest – oh, those depths again … those depths in people's lives …

Just before seven o'clock he drew level with the scoop. It was perhaps an arm's length above his head. It had stopped snowing and the wind had almost dropped. From time to time it burst out in little icy gusts, flickering up the powder snow along the whole length of the upper lip. It was bitterly cold. A general gloom obscured the upper face. It was so dark Raymond could only just make out the figure of his companion poised there below the scoop, clipping into a peg, stepping up into a sling. He saw a head poke up, black against the grey snow, and an arm raised, and the axe descend. Then, a split second later, a long despairing cry echoed over the face.

He knew that what he feared most had happened. The ledge was not a ledge at all. It was useless. He saw that Daniel had slumped forward across the edge of the scoop, his head against the snow. He must have dropped his hammer. It was swinging at the end of its loop, knocking against the rock. Raymond heard it – tap – tap – tap … Then it, too, stopped.

For a long time he looked up at the dark shape huddled against the face, willing it to come to life again. But Daniel never moved. And Raymond knew that there was nothing he could do. In different circumstances, with another man he might have raged – threatened – screamed obscenities – anything … But these things were useless here. He knew what Daniel was suffering now: knew, too, that no one could help him.

And so he waited patiently, in silence, for the outcome of the struggle that Daniel had to fight with himself.

Minutes passed and there was no movement. No sign of life. At length he looked up past the dark figure against the patch of snow, up into the gloom where the face and the sky merged blankly into one grey bank of darkening mist. If there's anybody up there, he thought despairingly, for Christ's sake help.

'You must climb,' he called. 'If ever you want to see them again you must climb now. Do you understand? You must climb now!' He heard the sound of his own voice echoing forlornly over the expanse of rock. The phrases merging, fading, dying away across the void. But he went on calling: calling Daniel's name, again and again, sometimes angrily, sometimes with great gentleness, as if he were calling to a child, all the time bending his mind towards the dark, motionless figure, straining his eyes up into the mist, willing him to move again.

'There will be another ledge,' he shouted. 'A good one. I know it. But you must look for it. We're relying on you. We're all relying on you.'

So, at half-past seven, Daniel moved at last. He stood upright in the sling. Raymond watched him step down from the useless sloping shelf and start once more up the lip of the fissure. At length he disappeared into the mist.

There was another ledge. But it took Daniel almost an hour to reach it, and another hour to bring up Raymond, and it was so small and narrow they had to sit wedged together with their legs dangling over the face, and so shelving that only the pegs, planted in the rock behind them, held them and their gear from sliding off. They could not cook. They could not even use the bivouac sac. Instead, they draped it over their bodies to keep out the wind and the snow which drove in at them again. It settled on them like a shroud.

Daniel was near collapse. He seemed only half aware of what was happening, slumped against Raymond, complaining monotonously.

Eventually he stopped. He was silent for so long Raymond thought he was asleep. But suddenly he sat bolt upright. He put both hands on the ledge and made as if to step down into space.

Christ! Raymond flung out his good arm and hauled him back.

'It's the glacier,' said Daniel excitedly. 'It's come up to meet us. Look! There!'

He pointed into the mist and strained forward but was hauled back again.

'For Christ's sake!' cried Raymond.

Daniel stared fixedly into the darkness while Raymond held on to him grimly.

'No,' he said eventually. 'It's not there. I thought it was there.'

He closed his eyes and slumped back against the rock.

Got to get a grip, he told himself. Keep awake. Sing! We're here because we're here because we're here because we're here.

But he felt himself going again … slipping away. Trembling, he gripped the edge of rock. In the Albergo Montebello, he thought, the old men will abuse us. He felt Raymond fumbling for something at his side. He thought of the guides, their hard, emphatic voices: 'There is nothing we can do.' Raymond had found the sling and was knotting it with one hand and his teeth.

CLIMBERS TRAPPED ON KILLER PEAK! That's how it will begin, he thought. Down there. That's how it starts. Reporters in the village. Camera crews. Technicians laying cable. Producers studying diagrams, cursing the weather.

Raymond slipped the knot into a karabiner and felt for the peg behind his back.

On the verandah of the small hotel – he thought of the boy's face at the window – maybe they will fix a telescope. Fifty centimes! Fifty centimes for a look. When the clouds lift all eyes turn to the face. *Viva! Viva la morte! Vive la mort!* Maybe in Munich, he thought, in Chamonix, a handful of men will hear the news. Will pack their gear and come south, remembering what it's like to die.

Raymond leaned across with a karabiner in his hand and roped for the peg at Daniel's side. Then he drew the sling tight through the karabiner, tight over his companion's chest, and back to his own peg.

'There!' he said, with satisfaction. 'That'll do it!'

He put his good arm across Daniel's shoulders and held him securely. *Tous les grands chefs*, thought Daniel sleepily, come quickly. Come for us soon … for the north wall candidates … for those swept by avalanche … struck by lightning … caught by stonefall in the unprotected couloir … dying of exposure … Holy Mary, Mother of God, pray, for all that fall …

He was asleep. From time to time he groaned, shifting against Raymond's good arm.

He's dreaming, thought Raymond.

But not of the acrobats: no – he dreamed of a place he'd never seen before, where mountains towered over corries of broom and heather: there were foxes there, and trout under dark stones in the frothy stream; no snow … no snow … but soft rain falling in the night on granite ridges which he never climbed. He sat alone on a beach of silver sand … he buried his legs in the sand … covered his thighs with a mound of silver sand …

I shall lose this arm at least, thought Raymond.

But Daniel moved in a lane overhung with branches: the quiet trees spread over him on either side, between the shadows the sun glared back in patches from the road, and a small black and white bird darted ahead of him down the lane, swerving silently from side to side in front of him.

If I lose nothing else, Raymond concluded, I shall lose this arm.

But for the moment the only thing that mattered was the ordeal of the night ahead. Reluctantly he fixed his mind upon it: reluctantly, because he was exhausted – because he knew the effort it would cost him – because at this moment he was thinking, maybe this time it will be the end. He would not talk, or sing, or force his thoughts on happier memories. He would bend with the cold. He would let the snow pile up above him. He would shrink to a small hard centre of resistance. And when dawn came round he might still be there.

Hour after hour he sat like that, with his good arm around Daniel's shoulders, drawing his companion's body into his own bulk and strength, enduring the dreadful cold and the icy grip of the darkness. Whether he passed out or not, or slept, he didn't know. His mind wandered back through years of incident: of great faces he had climbed, or nearly died on, of men he'd known or known of – hard men like himself. All the north wall candidates.

All of them had come to this in the end.

Some wore the medal of St Christopher. Some preferred a rabbit's foot, worn *pour la bonne chance*. Some carried transistor radios, to hear reports of the weather. Some studied the sky for a sign. Some put their trust in protective clothing, in clothing, in fibreglass helmets. Some tied intricate knots. Some fought the storm with hammers, with pegs driven deep. Some clung to the face in slings, sitting in étriers. Some sought to prolong life with screws, jammed nuts, expansion bolts, karabiners, channels, golos. Some punched holes in the ice, clawed pockets ringed with blood. Some fought with axes till the shafts snapped. They clutched at the rescue that never came.

But some survived for a while. Grew middle-aged. Saw their children marry. Lived to take their grandsons up to the huts on Sunday afternoons in summer, to shake hands with the guardian, to point out the routes they'd climbed. Like veterans of the war. The lucky ones, for whom all wounds have healed. So the catastrophes one has survived become things to smile about. And the children never ask, '*Grand-Père*? Who died there instead of you?'

But if they did, what would one say? That there, by the Klan there, the great guide Magand watched his brother dying in the snow – saw three of his friends die, one by one, in the snow – and could do nothing.

It was his fifth night on the face. And he remembered how he'd spent his fifth night on the north face of the Plan, in the bitter knowledge that he'd delayed too long, that they would have descended many hours earlier, that the weather would not break and that now, whatever happened, at first light they must get away, they must get to the Requin. But while he waited on his own strength, they had already shrunk beneath the limit of resistance, had already passed the furthest point from which one can return. He could not have known how close they were to death. And so at dawn he'd led them out, weakened as they were, down through the most savage blizzard he had ever known, through snow waist-deep at times, driving them mercilessly because he still had strength and they had not. And four of them had died.

He heard again the voices calling faintly through the wild shrieking of the storm, felt his own despair and fury rising as he turned back into the wind, trudged back to the sérac saw the torchlight, the little group of comrades, and Guérin plunging clumsily towards him – 'it's André – he's dying'.

The hours passed. But never for a moment did he loosen his grip around Daniel's shoulders until the first, faint bars of light showed out from the face. Then he realised that it was the eighteenth of August at last, and somewhere out there, beyond the mist, the sun was coming up again.

And he relaxed, knowing they had survived, and he fell asleep.

11　Chapter 11

'Look!' said Raymond.

He tried again, patiently but emphatically.

'It's the obvious thing to do,' he said. 'It would save at least seventy metres.'

I'm freezing to death, thought Daniel. He sat in a stupor on the ledge. It was as if he'd sat all night on a block of ice. He had no feelings in his thighs or buttocks. He dug his nails hard into his fingertips and felt no pain. Both his feet seemed dead. When he kicked the toes of his boots together he felt nothing.

'Twenty metres at the most,' said Raymond persuasively. 'A traverse of twenty metres.'

Daniel stared mutely into space. For the first time in three days he could see the spires and turrets of the Zoccone spur across the glacier. He watched them coming and going eerily in the mist. Overhead the sky was leaden. The cloud boiled silently on the glacier 1,000 metres down. It coiled like smoke among the rocks.

Les Merveilles du monde sauvage, he thought. Something like that. A thick brown book with a torn spine and heavy covers. And yet, a book of marvels. Marvellous names and pictures. Patagonia – range upon range of desolate spines and stacks. One like an arrowhead – or a spearblade in the cloud.

Must have been Cerro Torre, he thought. Hammered everlastingly. Perhaps the worst place in the world. I'll go there one day, he'd said …

'We could reach the corner in a couple of hours,' Raymond urged. 'And then we are not much more than 150 metres from the top.'

You're lying, thought Daniel, sourly.

He looked without enthusiasm at the crack. It began at the ledge on which he sat, and ran upwards across the wall. A thin crack marked by a flimsy line of snow that vanished at the dièdre. There was nothing else.

In childhood, he thought, everything is possible. Even at the other end of the world. Even Cerro Torre and the Towers of Paine. He'd never go there now. And it occurred to him that he'd never really accepted that idea before – that there were places in the world he'd never see. No one had ever asked him. And if they had he would have shrugged and said – Yes, there are places I shall never see – without any sense of being diminished. No one could name those places without, in a sense, making them available. To be born is to inherit any part of the world one chooses. But to realise one will never go there …

Like making a will, he thought. That was something else he hadn't done.

'Twenty metres,' Raymond pleaded. 'Only twenty metres. And it could save us hours.'

He's right, thought Daniel. It was true. A twenty-metre traverse into the dièdre (if it existed) would cut the distance to the corner by half. Seventy metres, certainly. And today every hour would count. And every metre. He looked again at the crack. It was perhaps twelve metres to the edge of the wall. Perhaps eight more into the dièdre itself (if Raymond had guessed right). If the crack went that far …

He tried to work it out. Perhaps twelve metres to the edge of the wall. Maybe an hour's work. Ten or twelve pegs, he thought.

'It would do no harm to take a look,' said Raymond. 'It's not far. It wouldn't take much effort.'

But now a hushed, chilly breeze began to blow against them. The wind was rising again. And the mist rose with it, drawn in a sudden up-current of air, rushing against the Zoccone spur opposite, submerging all but the topmost ridge of rock that ran now like a parapet along the length of cloud.

'All right!' said Daniel eventually. 'I'll go.'

But it took an immense effort of will to reach for his equipment, to shift limbs stiffened after hours of cramped, frozen confinement on the tiny ledge – an immense effort even to bring himself to move at all. For some minutes he sat on in silence staring out towards the Zoccone spur. He saw the cloud massing behind the long parapet of rock; a long grey line of men, he thought, weary, frightened like himself, waiting to begin the dawn attack.

'What time is it?' he asked.

'Just before six o'clock.'

'I'll go at six.'

'At six, then.'

A few moments later, as if in answer to a score of whistles blown along the line, the grey regiment rose over the parapet and rolled slowly towards the face.

'It's six now,' said Raymond.

Daniel reached for his hammer. And though he'd grown accustomed to privations, though nothing came more readily now than this daily struggle for survival, for him to leave that tiny, icy ledge called for the utmost act of courage. It was like stepping off the edge' of the world. Advancing into a swaying, tottering, lurching universe of creaking ropes, and icy metal things that clicked and clattered between frozen fingers, in which the last vestiges of sensitive touch were all but deadened by the gloves he wore. Movement was a frantic, hampered scuffle: fumbling to get boots into the nylon loops, treading the air like loose sand, hanging from stiffened limbs that ached under the load, clinging with one arm to the present, reaching for the next moment with the other, gasping the freezing air for breath under the strain.

And all the while the mist closed in around him. Gradually Raymond's figure diminished to a vague concentration of the cloud, and Daniel began to fear lest, when he reached the edge of the wall, he should not be able to see into the dièdre. And then a new fear struck him. A short horizontal traverse on pegs was one thing. But suppose the crack took a steep upward climb to the dièdre? It might take fifty metres to get there, for all he knew. He stopped for a few moments and rested, his body swaying in the tapes. He pressed his head against the gloved hands clutching the karabiner.

'Oh, God!' he muttered. 'Please don't let it be like that.'

The thought of soloing a pitch like that without direct aid from the rope appalled him. Not because it was impossible. It could be done. The *grands chefs* could climb like that. He thought of Bonatti, alone on the south-west pillar: of Barbier – all three north faces of the Tre Cima. It called for strength, speed, precision – and a cold, clear knowledge of oneself.

But he was lucky. The crack led straight to the dièdre. As he moved round the edge of the rock he saw a thin seam bisecting the stone, and the snow-choked line of the fault lying like a shadow down the intersection of the grey, opposing walls.

Then a bird flew out from the face. A bird!

Still shaken he watched it go. Into the wind it flew, slower and slower … until it hung there, poised, the forward thrust of its wings matching the wind exactly – then it turned in a tight, banking curve, and began to go up in the air, circling without effort on the updraught.

He clung with one hand to the karabiner and swung round to watch it climb. In summer larks went up like that at his feet – went up from little cups of grass. He bent all his heart and mind upon the climbing bird, followed it to where it hung for a moment – rolled sideways – then plunged down and disappeared.

The mist closed in behind it. But its passing seemed to leave a gap across the sky – an opening through which he saw dimensions of a larger world. It was a visionary moment. Something scarcely grasped. The acrobats of his childhood were still the same (secure, guiltless, they flew like birds between the bars). But his life lay in the encircling world beyond. It could not stop here, not at his fingertips, not at the boundaries of his nerves: it must flow as far as his eye could see, range as freely as his mind, rejoice in everything …

Perhaps that is why we have been reduced like this, he thought. Deprived of those we love – stripped of all certainty – of grace – of God even – so that we may learn what it is to be ourselves …

All this flashed upon him as the bird plunged out of sight. It lasted no more than moments. Then the hard, objective world came back at him through the mist. Rock, and ice, and snow.

For a moment everything had been revealed. Now it was gone. And what it was, he didn't know.

His thigh was hurting him. His wrist ached from gripping the karabiner. He became aware of a strange sound, thin and harsh, like the cry of an animal, dispersing over the huge expanse of rock. It was the sound of his own name.

He shuddered. It was bitterly cold.

'I'm here!' he shouted. 'It's all right. It'll go.'

He unclipped another peg with cold, reluctant fingers, stretched out, swaying in the loops, to place it and reached down for his hammer.

The traverse saved them over seventy metres. But it took them two hours to climb the remaining sixty metres to the corner.

A few metres above the traverse the angle of the fault fell back a little. It was still steep. But it sloped sufficiently for the falling snow to settle and offered an unstable lodging to whatever debris crashed down from the great corner. Ordinarily it would have been a difficult climb on good rock, with more or less ice according to conditions. But the huge avalanche three days earlier, and many hours of storm, had so affected the fault at this point that the whole character of the passage was transformed. The dièdre was no longer a roughly V-shaped corner, but a kind of gutter, like a steep scree gully, jammed with enormous blocks – whether of old snow, or ice, or rock, it was impossible to say since all were overlaid with fresh, or frozen, or partly frozen snow.

They kept close together, separated by no more than a few metres of rope at a time. Every three or four metres Daniel stopped, braced himself as best he could, and kept the rope tight enough to hold Raymond upright as he followed each step or handhold. For Daniel there could be no protection. The whole passage was unjustifiable. There was no technique to offer security in conditions such as these. The stability of the great blocks was always uncertain. The depth and texture of the snow crust varied at each step. Each movement was hazardous and had to be rehearsed, its particular nature anticipated, probed with the axe – gently at first, then gingerly with the boot – while the steel pick or spike quivered as Daniel pressed it hard against the snow, held his breath and shifted his weight into the move.

There were terrifying moments when his foot dropped suddenly, only to be checked by something lower down beneath the snow. And in the split second of panic between anticipation and relief he felt such a clutch of terror that each new movement left him progressively less able to withstand the shock of fear, while each firm foothold became a little island of security that he could scarcely bring himself to relinquish. So he alternated continuously between terror and relief. It was like a strange pathological obsession, or a nightmare in which the solid ground gives way at every step. He was climbing at the extreme edge of self-control, continually muttering piteous little prayers under his breath.

Eventually he stopped altogether. He turned to Raymond, grey and frozen-faced a few metres below.

'I think we should turn back,' he said gravely.

'We can't turn back,' said Raymond.

Daniel stared at him for a long moment. Then he raised his axe in an odd gesture of submission and turned back to the snow. Alarmed, Raymond watched him go. He won't get up, he thought.

But Daniel continued doggedly to hack a way up through the gully. Every few metres he stopped, made a stance and kept the rope tight for his companion. For a long time he said nothing. He seemed to have forgotten his anxiety over the condition of the snow. Then, suddenly, he began to complain of his feet. Each time Raymond came up to a stance, Daniel looked at him out of anxious eyes. His voice was frightened.

'I can't feel anything,' he said. 'I'm sure they're freezing … '

It was possible, thought Raymond. A bivouac in the open, sitting on icy rock, knees bent …

'Stamp them!' he said. 'Keep the blood moving!'

Whether or not Daniel's feet were frozen was of small importance beside his fear. That was what worried Raymond. Daniel was utterly convinced.

'I can feel them freezing,' he insisted.

'Wriggle your toes,' said Raymond.

He did so. But he kept forgetting. It was as if, in the grim concentration of the climb he could only think of one thing at a time, and he kept discovering that he was not wriggling his toes. Then it occurred to him that if they were frozen perhaps he wouldn't be able to tell whether he was wriggling them or not. This worried him more and more. Again he stopped and turned questioningly to Raymond.

'If I turned back,' he asked, 'what would you do?'

'I'd have to go on alone.' Raymond tried to keep the alarm out of his voice.

Daniel said nothing. He raised his axe once more in the gesture of acquiescence and began again up the gully. After a few minutes he stopped in a narrow place, between a huge block and the back of the dièdre, crouched, took off his outer windproof gloves and began to pull at the laces of his boot. Raymond thought he meant to slacken the straps of his crampons. But Daniel removed the crampon altogether and started to unlace his boot.

'No!' screamed Raymond. 'No! No!'

He scrambled frantically up the few metres of steep snow, stabbing desperate handholds with the pick of his hammer. When he came up just below the stance Daniel had removed one boot and was beginning on the other. His crampons, the boots and his gloves were piled precariously at the very edge of the snow slope.

'Got to rub them,' said Daniel calmly. 'They're freezing.'

Aghast at what he saw Raymond tried, none the less, to control his voice.

'No!' he said hurriedly. 'Not here!'

In his anxiety he made an involuntary movement of his broken arm to safe-guard the equipment and cried aloud at the sudden pain. Daniel must have thought him about to fall for he made a quick grab at the arm which held the hammer. His hand struck against the discarded boot, dislodging the gloves, which toppled on to Raymond's shoulder, rested there for a moment while he stared at them despairingly, then slid off into space.

Daniel watched them tumbling down the snow.

'Christ!' he said. 'Oh, God!'

Ten minutes later they climbed out of the gully and stopped to rest in the lit-tle snow basin at the foot of the great corner. They were less than 200 metres from the summit. Daniel peeled off his sodden, woollen gloves. He had to bite at the wool and drag them off between his teeth. His fingers were white and violet and numb. He raised them to his mouth. They had the touch of wax against his lips. He had forgotten about his feet. He sat miserably sucking his fingers one by one, too dazed to think of anything. But Raymond worked swiftly, rummaging in the big sac with one hand, pulling out the stove, the last bar of food, and all the spare socks he could find.

'Put these on,' he said.

Daniel stared uncomprehendingly at the red Cortina stockings.

'On your arms!' said Raymond.

He lit the stove and placed it between Daniel's knees, with a pan of snow on top.

'Look after this,' he said. 'Warm your hands. Make sure you don't burn them.'

Daniel did as he was told.

'You'll be all right,' said Raymond, thinking – he's got to get to the top – somehow he *must* get to the top.

And he sat wearily on the big sac and fumbled inside his duvet for the packet of Celtique.

Ultimately, he thought, it is the small disasters that destroy us.

He had one cigarette left. He lit it and surveyed the dièdre. It rose directly above a little ramp of frozen snow which inclined steeply from the basin where they were resting.

He looked up, and up … had to bend his head right back to see the top. Mist hung at the far end of it, shifting continually between the steep, grim walls. Even in the dismal light he could see the pale glint of ice in the crack, and thin patches of verglas, like wet stains on the walls. The great corner. Most of it ver-tical, or overhanging: 100 metres high.

Forgetting the loss of Daniel's gloves, forgetting his own injuries, he smoked and gazed, totally absorbed, enacting in his mind the moves that must have carried the Italians so many years before. Each man silent, intimidated, and those tremendous walls streaming with water … After three days on the face one would not be cheered by such a sight. He imagined Schiavi on the long overhanging layback at the top. Gripped, sweating, his strength going, praying for a place to rest, finding nothing, never stopping, feet pushing, hands crossing in the crack, hauling on the fingers, gasping 'fight it! fight it!' every overhanging metre of the way until the top. Now three of them were dead. And Schiavi finished. Only the corner remained – huge, empty, streaked with ice. Just as they had found it years earlier, offering now the same grim struggle it had offered then.

Raymond saw it all. He felt a profound respect for them, for the dead Italians. For all the north wall candidates he felt a profound respect. And he was glad he'd never married, or served tourists in a small hotel, or kept a shop. Despite all the deaths, despite everything, he was glad he was as he was. Grateful. He looked up in wonder at the great pitch, and wished desperately that he could lead it now.

Daniel sat with his back to the wind, his hands curled around the stove. If he raised his hand the flame wavered, its noise faltered. At school they had always been hungry. In the spring, sometimes, he used to go with Denis to the monks' garden after supper and eat the radishes which grew there. He'd never confessed it. He used to think that stealing was taking something to offend Our Lord, and he would never have done that deliberately. So no one had ever known. And that was strange because Brother Michael kept the garden. He must have known. He must have known and said nothing. He thought of Brother Michael leading the crocodile of little boys on Sunday afternoons in summer ... along the Rue Michelet ... the Jardin des Allées ... down the steep steps by the Church of the Sacred Heart, his soutane swishing over the cobbles of the Place Kléber, where the village boys ran alongside him shrieking 'Bonjour madame! Bonjour madame!' – and Denis stepping out, fists clenched, threatening ...

Daniel rocked gently backwards and forwards over the stove. Ah, Denis, Denis ...

The stew stuck glutinously to the spoon. Raymond scraped it off against the side of the pan and offered it.

'Take it!' he said.

But Daniel seemed not to notice. He sat without moving, staring straight ahead at the rock.

It was beginning to snow again. Raymond withdrew the pan. It was cooling rapidly in the bitter air. A thin glaze had formed already over the brown surface of the stew. A few flakes of snow settled there. Raymond sheltered it against his body and looked down wearily.

'What's the matter?'

Daniel sat without any movement of the eyes; his face still set rigidly to the rock.

'I do not understand you,' said Raymond. 'I don't know what's the matter with you. Whatever it is, you must put it out of your mind.'

He spoke simply, quietly, but with great earnestness.

'We have been lucky,' he said. 'Do you realise that? Very lucky. We are still alive. If we can climb this corner we may get off with our lives. Perhaps there will be amputations. Perhaps I shall lose this arm. Maybe you will lose toes and fingers, I don't know. But we shall have survived. We shall live!'

His voice rose emphatically with the last few words. Then he paused. He looked directly at Daniel.

'It is our duty at least to try to get away,' he said.

He hesitated. Then added, simply, 'I cannot do it without you.'

Daniel kept silence for so long that Raymond gave up hope of a reply. He looked away in despair – then turned, and gripped him with his good hand and shook him vigorously.

'You don't understand,' he said fiercely. 'We must *get away*. We *must* get away.'

But it took him almost half an hour to restore in Daniel the necessary sense of purpose, to induce him to eat, to make preparations, to study the corner. And even though he listened carefully to everything his companion said, he said nothing himself but stood nodding briefly – not looking at the corner but staring down at the snow, stroking the butt of his peg hammer with stiff fingers. Eventually, subdued and silent, his hands encased in the wet woollen gloves again, he kicked his way slowly up the steep ramp of frozen snow towards the towering line of the corner.

'Remember!' Raymond shouted anxiously. 'Think what you're going to do – then go fast!'

If you exist, he prayed, for Christ's sake look after him. Keep him safe.

Somewhere, somehow, there should be something that might offer Daniel the protection he could no longer give.

'Jam whenever you can!' he shouted. 'Keep going!'

Twice within the first few minutes Daniel fell. He fell twice from the same position, the awkward bulge on the short wall at the foot of the corner. He did not fall far. But the second time he landed badly and was so shaken that he slid almost the entire length of the ramp before he could get the long pick of his hammer into the snow. He came to rest at the bottom of the basin, almost at Raymond's feet, grey faced and gasping. Raymond helped him up again. He was covered with snow. There was blood above the icy fringe of his beard.

'Verglas!' he gasped, … can't get a grip … skid straight off the wall.'

'Jam it!' said Raymond.

'Can't feel anything. I just can't feel anything.'

Nevertheless, at the next attempt, he tried to jam it, thrusting both hands deep into the fault, twisting and dragging them until they were wedged tight between the gritty walls of the crack. The jams held.

Slowly he climbed from under the bulge, up on to the slight shoulder above it, where he rested for a moment with his fists still wedged in the crack. There he rested, breathing heavily, conscious of his heart pounding after the strenuous effort, with trickles of fresh blood from the cuts and lacerations drying on his face. Just above him the corner sloped inward slightly for three or four metres, following the line of the shoulder on which he stood, then rose straight as the side of a house to the next stance almost twenty-five metres overhead.

He stared upwards. A long, long way above him the mist seemed to rise and fall constantly, an endless motion of vague comings and goings. He strained his eyes to follow each indefinite eddy, hoping to see the top of the corner. He felt the snow settling on his nose and cheeks, and heard the solemn, melancholy noise the wind makes between great walls – but he could see only an endlessly shifting and merging grey vista of rock and mist. He looked down. The doubled rope fell in twin curves to Raymond thirty metres below, and beyond him was the mist, and beneath the mist … 1,000 metres through the empty air … the glacier, the valley and the world of men.

Lodged there, in a precarious stance on the sloping shoulder above the bulge Daniel experienced a strange feeling that he had arrived at last at the crucial place.

As he began his preparations for bringing up Raymond he felt beyond any further doubt or hope that he was going to die. He had known it all his life. He had come face to face with it three days earlier at the very moment his eyes had lit on the line of that black cloud. The initial disbelief and the clutch of panic he had felt then was the shock of recognition. And for three days he had practised the gestures, rehearsed the attitudes and explored the various pretensions with which he might face the termination of a life as commonplace as anybody's life.

Now he knew that nothing was required. No gestures, no attitudes, no pretensions, nothing at all. Yet it did not strike him as ironic that in the corner he would be called upon to make a desperate fight for life. It was simply something he had to do. Something that had to be concluded.

He had great difficulty in preparing the belay. He had to clear the crack of ice and place the piton with fingers that seemed to close on nothing. It was not until he saw strips of raw flesh between the tears in his gloves that he realised just how fiercely he had wedged them in the crack. Yet he felt only slight pain. The gloves were dirty and ragged now, and stained with fresh blood. He felt a distant, objective pity for his hands. More than anything he was immensely sorry. As he took in the ropes he felt immensely sorry. He thought of them, but they seemed to merge into one composite figure, child and woman, solid, like something carved in stone. He thought of them all the time, but he kept the ropes tight, and his eyes on Raymond. He felt no alarm. When Raymond arrived Daniel listened placidly to all he had to say, all the while studying the corner, wondering how far he would get before he fell.

Almost certainly he would have fallen had it not been for the pegs. At first he couldn't bring himself to trust them. When he saw the first, at thirty metres, just below the second stance, he didn't believe it was really there. Even when he'd clipped into it he couldn't bring himself to trust it and for several seconds he hesitated, bridging the crack with feet on either wall, before he moved his weight on to the sling. After that, at the worst places, whenever he was in trouble, almost at the point of failure, there was a peg. Below the swing under the overhang at forty metres, under the steep wall that led to the niche, at all the worst places there were pegs. There were four of them on the long overhanging layback at the top. Eventually he came to accept them, wondering neither who had placed them nor how long they had been there, simply clipping into each peg as it came towards him, resting, and leaving it behind him as he passed on his way.

But the condition of his hands worsened steadily. Familiar things he had handled half his life seemed to lose their shape, their hard identifying outlines melting the instant that he touched them. He had to push open the spring-loaded gates in the karabiners with the bottom joints of his fingers. He used his fists like wooden wedges on each jam, wrenching them into friction with the rock to make sure they held. Although they were badly mangled they didn't bleed much now, but the sight of them sickened him. He tried not to look at them. Yet he felt only a little pain.

Undoubtedly it was the pegs that kept him alive. And, as he climbed higher and higher up the great corner (and because he hadn't fallen yet), he began to think in terms of going further. Not of going home, or of getting to the hut. Not for a moment did he cease to feel that he was going to die. Yet he thought he might get further.

When I get to the top, he told himself (the top seemed an appropriate place), I'll sit down.

And so he concentrated all his energies on getting to the top. But it was the pegs that kept him alive. On the long, gruelling layback which concluded the diedre, even with four pegs to rest at, he suffered a terrible diminution of his strength.

And so he came at last to the twin chimneys, the natural exit from the face. He was utterly exhausted – and so disorientated he was quite unable to choose which line to follow. When Raymond arrived he found Daniel gazing upward in bewilderment.

'I'm not at all sure about this,' he told Raymond. 'I don't like this at all.'

The twin chimneys were really one huge snow gully split through almost its entire length by a narrow projecting buttress. The gully was less than fifty metres long but very steep, much steeper than any roof, with a dangerous, heavily corniced exit. From below it looked vertical.

'We must keep going,' said Raymond.

Daniel remembered that he had to get to the top. Doubtfully, with much grumbling he began up the left-hand branch. For some metres he struggled upwards, slipping at almost every step in fresh powder snow a few centimetres thick that squeaked uneasily and slid down against the old, hard-packed *névé* underneath.

It's not on, he told himself.

It was hopeless. He came down.

'Try the other,' he muttered.

'The snow'll be just the same … ' began Raymond.

'Try it anyway,' said Daniel.

It was just the same. He had to cut through the powder and chip steps in the *névé*. At every blow his face was sprayed with ice. It took a long time and much effort because he was forced to cut left-handed. The fingers of his right hand lacked all sensation. They were dead already. He was clumsy and wasted much of the little strength left to him with crude, inaccurate blows of the adze. He was well aware of it, knew his performance was falling short of what was required, and it worried him. He began to think he might not get to the summit. At every halt Raymond drove him on.

'We must keep going,' he said.

And Daniel knew he must keep going.

When I get to the summit, he told himself, I can let myself go. I can lie down. I can go to sleep.

But he had to get to the summit.

Cutting steps up the gully required an enormous effort. The steady, regular rise and fall of the adze gave way to a jerky, exhausted hacking at the ice. In the intervals between each spasmodic burst of activity he bent double over the axe, sometimes for minutes on end, gasping, so that it took longer and longer to cut each step. He was well aware of what was happening. He knew very well that his feet were freezing. But they were a long way off at the other end of his body. And though the fear of not getting to the top was a constant anxiety, since that was now the only aim he had, yet the malfunction of his body continually interposed itself between his mind and its objective. From time to time he stumbled across a consciousness that seemed not his own, as if it was someone else and not himself absorbed in the glint of the axe head as the yellow shaft flashed at the ice. And then he had to fetch the adze back from the line of little chips on which it had embarked. He was mesmerised by the sight of that jerky arm, no longer under his control, that rose and fell of its own accord. Spasmodically it hacked at the ice. It seemed to practise, in a crude beginner's way, its recent, fresh-won separation from the body. Like the twitching limb of something killed …

In his bewildered state he found himself driven back, protesting and frightened, back along the Rue de la Gare to that shop from which, as a child, he half-averted his eyes whenever he passed by. But now its window was alive with snapping, jerking, clicking horrors in glossy plastic and padded leather, rimmed with stainless steel, with steel buckles and bright yellow leather straps that clicked and creaked and wheezed merrily.

'Fight it!' shouted Raymond. 'Keep going!'

Whenever Daniel's progress seemed to falter Raymond drove him on. He, too, was near exhaustion. He had entered once again into the survival area – the territory of the desperate fight for life. But the summit was very close now. And the hut was only two hours beyond the summit. Once at the summit he could take control. He could lead them both down the *Voie Normale*. He could drag Daniel to the hut. But they must get to the summit. He kept close to Daniel, never more than a few metres behind, and drove him on relentlessly because he had to. Whatever happened they must not stop; they must not sit down. At all costs they must keep going.

Just after two o'clock they arrived at the head of the gully. Under the strong eddies and cross-currents at the top of the face the snow seemed to be cast in all directions, as the wind whirled in from every side, battering the two men with fierce flurries of hail. Daniel halted on the steep ice slope a few metres ahead of Raymond. Immediately above him the cornice jutted out into the gully. It hung in the air like an enormous wave, frozen, its underside jagged and grimy, pitted with craters and blackened by meltwater where it lay up against the rock. A small part of it had collapsed already, leaving a narrow vertical chimney between the frozen snow and the icy wall of the gully.

Raymond looked up at the tons of unsupported snow poised overhead and waited (he was feeling faint again ... terrified of fainting now) while Daniel cut his way up the back of the gully, until he was directly underneath the cornice with the open mouth of the chimney no more than a metre above his head. There he paused and closed his eyes for a moment, and gathered himself for the final assault.

When his eyes opened again he experienced a moment of complete lucidity, of absolute detachment. Below him the icy slope of the gully fell away, dropped away to infinity ... He looked up. As if for the first time in six days he saw the sky, grey and implacable, like light at the end of a long tunnel, and walls of snow curving backwards towards the summit. Calmly he looked for a place to put the piton.

This, he told himself, will be the last ... the last one.

He felt no pain from the various cuts and lacerations on his face. His hands no longer hurt at all. His right hand, up to the wrist, was like a block of wood. He could still move the fingers (but stiffly ... very stiffly), and though they served to steady the peg in the crack he couldn't feel what they held. Twice he struck his hand. He saw the grey, swollen glove sink in under the hammerhead. But he felt nothing. Several times he missed the peg altogether and struck the rock.

It took a long time to place the piton. At the last blow the haft of the hammer snapped clean across the line of the steel shank. The head dropped like a stone into the snow. He looked at the piece of wood he held in his hand. *Fabriqué par J.N.* – twelve years he'd carried it. He tossed it away down the gully. He saw it strike the steep slope many metres below and bounce out into the mist.

All around him the snow was falling straight down, softly, in big flakes. He saw the flakes falling but he couldn't feel them. They fell without a sound, straight down, as if the wind had stopped. He felt very tired. He looked down at Raymond and jerked his head towards the broken cornice.

'Almost there,' he said.

Wearily Raymond climbed the steps in the steep slope while Daniel did his best to keep the rope tight. His hands were almost useless. There was blood on the snow, and blood streaked along the rope. The glove that held it was black with blood. When Raymond saw Daniel's hands he opened his mouth to speak, but could say nothing. He only shook his head. Daniel turned in towards the chimney and tried to force his way up between the narrow, icy walls. But he was so weak, and his hands and feet were so crippled that he could make very little progress until Raymond got beneath, painfully, and heaved him up towards the snowfield. He disappeared over the lip of the cornice. Raymond sank back and watched the bloodied rope slithering up after him, sickened.

But Daniel felt no alarm at all. He was thinking of all the saints in coloured lights in the great east window. In red and blue, mostly. Some in a rich yellow. One in deep green. Here at the summit there was no colour other than the grey sky and the colour of the snow falling interminably, snow and sky together. *Tous les grands chefs.* Shepherds, poor woodcarvers, crystal gatherers, hunters of chamois. They were changed now. They wore their incorruptible garments now. Transfigured perpetually they lived in a state of grace before all things. But he knew them all the same. Those grave bearded faces. Melchior Anderegg (still with a coil of rope, he saw) huge and stern, like Moses before the tribes – and in the tree the little one they called *der Gletscherwolf* because of his long loping stride. He looked everywhere for Maquignaz' thin, bandit face. But he couldn't see him anywhere. He'll be there somewhere, he thought, he's bound to be there …

The steep white slope flowed bumpily down towards him, and he floated over it in a dream. But there was still something that held him down, that stopped him veering off to the side. He was glad of that. He had to get to the summit. Yes … he'll be there somewhere, he thought; they were all there … in the great east window above the altar. And in their midst, enthroned in red and blue, *Notre Dame de la Belle Verriére*, her thin white arms folded around the child. The child wore a heavy headdress that was familiar. He'd seen it before. He knew it! Was it the child's face staring from the window … or his child … or was it her face looking out at him? His grandmother's? And was he, then, the child … He didn't know. It no longer mattered. For she sat not looking down at the child but outwards, at all who would look at her, the pale, kind face resolving all complexities. Above her head, with outstretched wings, rose the lark in the song his grandmother sang, going up … up … in the morning, with the dew all on its breast.

If this is the end of everything, he thought … if there is nothing more than this …

He felt enormously relieved. To know, he thought, to *know*, after all that has happened to us …

He was weightless now. He felt nothing. It was all so effortless. He seemed to stand aside from his body. His legs, below the knees, had disappeared altogether, but there was still something that held him down, that anchored him, that kept him at the level of the snow. And he was angry. He wanted to be off. He became aware of the ice axe rising and falling. He noticed the shaft of the ice axe just in front of him. It rose and fell jerkily at the end of his arm, driving into the snow, and he decided that it was the ice axe that kept him down. If he let go of it he would float away. But he couldn't release it. He couldn't open his fingers. His eyes filled with tears. He was overcome with desolation. Then he remembered that he had to get to the summit.

So he plunged on up the slope. The shaft of the axe rose and fell irregularly. He saw it driving into the snow, but he couldn't hear it. His ears seemed to be stuffed with cotton wool, behind which a ponderous, rapid thumping blotted out all other sounds. He couldn't even hear the song about the lark. But he could still see it, soaring up above familiar fields, hanging above the pine woods … All at once he smelt the strong scent of resin from the deep bed of crushed cones and needles at his feet. And he felt an enormous happiness welling up … like the lark, singing like the lark; not the happiness of comradeship, but the astonishing happiness of entering a marvellous new land (oh, ferns … butterflies … so many things) with that image of the lark in the morning going up … up … before him into the clean air, leading him as he staggered knee-deep through the wet, sluggish snow, until he neared the crest of the slope where he was met by a fierce wind beating at his face, battering his chest and shoulders, tearing at his clothes, gathering him into it step by step until it embraced him wholly, and then he sighed and closed his eyes and sank down at last into the snow.

All the way up Raymond knew that the slope might avalanche at any second. It was bitterly cold. He heard the wind blowing above him with a harsh, dry sound but he couldn't feel it yet. He scarcely noticed the rope slanting down towards him through the falling snow, dark and solid, quivering like a hawser, drawing him up, safeguarding him at every step. He was exhausted, but his strange will (a kind of cold, controlling centre – and so indifferent it seemed a thing apart) drove him on. He knew he must keep going, and trudged on, thrusting the shaft of the north wall hammer before him like a blind man's staff. Before him was a clumsy stumbling track, as if a large wounded animal had trampled through the thick wet snow. It wound from side to side across the slope.

As he drew nearer the summit the sound of the wind grew louder and more harsh. And behind it he heard another sound, tuneless and spasmodic, rising and falling erratically, coming and going through the wind: it was Daniel singing.

There in the window was the mystery blazing in the midst, with faces of angels all around, and the *grands chefs* singing Jaro's hymn ...

Daniel's cracked voice pierced weirdly through the gusts of wind. He sat just below the summit, like a child sitting on a beach, with his legs and thighs buried in the snow. He was belayed to the ice axe and was taking in Raymond's rope. Most of the glove had gone from the right hand. Bits of it remained, scabs of blackened wool stuck to the flesh. The hand itself never left the rope. As he took it in he simply dragged the rope through the clenched, frozen fist, stripping away flesh and wool together at every pull. He lifted a frightful face towards Raymond, looked at him out of one eye – for the other was frozen shut – and grinned.

'We're there!' he said.

His beard and eyebrows were white with frost. Apart from the blackened areas of dried blood the rest of his face was bloodless. White dead skin peeled from his nose and lips. Only the one, dark hollow eye blinked in a dead face.

He should look after that hand, Raymond thought instinctively. He ought to save those bits of skin. Then he realised. It was as if he sensed the north wall candidates of twenty years gathering like ghosts around him in the snow.

C'est lui qui mourra! they whispered, *c'est lui qui mourra!*

He knew. He knew for certain that, once again, he must suffer another survival, endure another death. He looked with awe and fear at the snow-shrouded figure grinning up at him from the snow.

'It's all over,' it said.

It smiled.

'It's finished!' it said.

'No!' said Raymond, gently. 'No, it's not finished. Not yet. We must get to the hut. We must keep going.'

'Going? I'm not going anywhere. You go!'

'No!' said Raymond. 'We've got to go together.'

'You will have it, won't you? You will have it so.'

Daniel paused. He looked away.

'You frighten me,' he said. 'You know? You and your go – you frighten me. You'd go on for ever if you could.'

He tried to get up but he couldn't. He tried and tried but he couldn't. His legs wouldn't move.

'It's no use,' he gasped. 'You go! I'll wait here. You go!'

Raymond put his good arm under Daniel's shoulders and tried to haul him to his feet. But it was useless. He kept falling down again.

'No use,' he gasped. 'You go!'

Raymond knelt beside him and began to massage his legs with one hand, rubbing and pummelling frantically, gasping for breath in his efforts to get the blood moving again. But it made no difference. After a while Daniel toppled sideways. But Raymond kept on trying. He wouldn't give up.

'Please,' he muttered between breaths, rubbing desperately, 'please – oh, please … '

And he began to weep.

When they arrived they found him still on his knees, rubbing the frozen legs. Daniel's body was almost covered by the silent, still falling snow. Raymond looked up as they approached.

'I didn't want this to happen,' he said to them. 'I didn't want it to be like this.'

He let them fasten him to the stretcher, but when he saw Jaro and Lino Casaletti unpacking the canvas shroud (kind Lino's face filled with distress –'poor man,' he was saying, 'poor, poor man') he gave a terrible cry and started up against the straps. Weak though he was they had to hold him while Tomas prepared the hypodermic.

After that he quietened. He called once for Belmonte, the young tiger, but Jean-Louis was fighting his own battle on the Grandes Jorasses. There was no one there from his own country, no one who spoke his language, so he had to tell it in German, clutching at the arm of the man who stood above him (it was Sepp Bohlen, come from Munich) as they jolted over the snow.

'Ich habe es nicht gewollt,' he kept saying. '*Ich habe es nicht gewollt.*'

Until he fell asleep.

Throughout the Alps the snow was general. Already it had closed about three Austrians on the ice fields of the Eiger. It was closing in for Belmonte, (his second night, now, on the Shroud). In the high meadows above Molino it fell as rain, where Luc Couzy and Roland Guiccioli, from Grenoble, were camped close to the Zoccone glacier. For three days they had been hemmed in by the rain. From time to time each man went out, barefooted, standing alone in the wet meadow, wondering at the deserted orange tent across the grass, or staring up at the mist hiding the face. But they could see nothing (and were, perhaps, relieved). Mostly they slept, or talked, or ate a little (for they hadn't much) and waited for the weather to lift.

Printed in the USA
CPSIA information can be obtained
at www.ICGtesting.com
JSHW012017140824
68134JS00025B/2459

9 781912 560578